NUDIST CAMP

First published in 1957
This edition published in 2024
by Wolfbait Books
www.wolfbait.co.uk
All rights reserved © 2024.

Cover design: Scott Sugiuchi
www.scottsugiuchi.com
Typeset by Theo Powney.

A CIP record for this book is available from the British Library
ISBN: 978-1-917298-07-0 (paperback)
ISBN: 978-1-917298-08-7 (ebook)

Paradise Has It's Price

NUDIST CAMP

by Orrie Hitt

FOREWORD

DEAR READER, YOU are holding a classic example of mid-20th-century American pulp fiction in your hands: *Nudist Camp,* written by the prolific and often underappreciated author Orrie Hitt.

Born in 1916 in the small town of Colchester (now Roscoe), New York, Hitt was a literary force of nature. This happily married father of four wrote around 150 books, and at the height of his career he was churning out one title every two weeks. His incredible output and keen observations of working-class America earned him the moniker "The Shakespeare of Shabby Street."

Despite leading a wholesome family life, Hitt's novels explored the gritty underbelly of American society, delving into themes of lust, greed, and the struggles of the working class to make ends meet. From insurance salesmen to auto mechanics, waitresses to dance hall girls, Hitt's characters were often just one bad decision away from disaster—or one good romp away from momentary bliss.

Nudist Camp was first published in 1957, at a time when Western society was caught between the conservatism of the post-war era and the stirrings of the sexual revolution that would explode in the following decade. In this cultural landscape, the concept of nudist camps held a particular fascination for the American public. These communities promised a return to nature and a rejection of society's constraints. In the popular imagination they came with the suggestion of sexual freedom and taboo pleasures. Ever the astute observer of societal trends, Hitt recognized the subject matter's potential—he even visited a nudist camp to gather material. *Nudist Camp* is, in fact, one of his three nudist-themed works, the other two being *The Naked Flesh* and *My Wild Nights with Nine Nudists* (written under the pseudonym Kay Addams).

In typical Hitt style, there's more beneath the surface in *Nudist Camp* than you might expect. For modern readers, the novel offers more than a nostalgic trip to the past. It provides a fascinating window into the social mores and hidden desires of 1950s America. The tensions it explores, between freedom and constraint, desire and propriety, individual fulfillment and societal expectations, remain relevant today. While Hitt's writing style is direct and engaging, his unflinching portrayal of personal hardships and life's difficulties resonates in our current era of economic uncertainty and social change. There is a raw authenticity beneath the surface kitsch.

Readers can expect vivid descriptions, snappy dialogue, and a plot that moves at a breakneck pace.

So grab your sunscreen, leave your swimsuit behind, and get ready for a skyclad adventure as we pay a visit to the nudist camp.

Yahya El-Droubie
London

1

DELLA STEPPED OUT of the shower, water dripping from her skin and forming tiny pools on the pink tile. A soft knock sounded on the bathroom door. Della rubbed herself with a heavy towel. "I'll be out in a moment."

Ricky, she thought. No, not Ricky. Ricky wouldn't be guilty of coming home so early and, even if he did, he wouldn't knock on the door. He'd try to batter a hole in it with his foot.

"Oh, that's all right, Mrs. Farland. It's just me, Jennie. I only wanted—"

"I said I'd be right out, didn't I?"

There was a brief silence.

"Yes, Mrs. Farland," Jennie finally said. "I'll wait."

Della sighed and pulled the red bathing cap from her head. There was no doubt about what Jennie wanted. Permission to go to town, of course. She was getting pretty sick of Jennie running off every night. If the poor thing needed a man so badly why didn't she pick on Jack, the gardener? He was only in his forties and strong enough for anything. Or one of those farmer boys, especially that older one, down the road. Della sighed again. Maybe Jennie had found something in town that she liked. She certainly talked enough about her Sammy!

Della finished drying and tossed away the towel. Then she got another towel from over the sink and worked it down across the mirror on the door. Ricky probably was the most useless husband outside a cemetery but there was one thing Della had to admit—he sure as hell knew how to build a house for his wife. Full-length mirrors, that's what a girl needed. Full-length mirrors everywhere so that a girl could take a quick inventory of her assets whenever she pleased, assets which her husband claimed were frozen tighter than American dollars on deposit in the Bank of Iceland.

Della Farland stepped away a little from the mirror and smiled at what she saw.

Twenty-two, she thought, or was it twenty-three? No, Twenty-two. For heaven's sake, what was the matter with her, almost jumping a year like that? Maybe Ricky was right, maybe her nerves were on edge. And maybe it wasn't living up here in the mountains that was doing it; maybe after all there was something to what Ricky said, that they shouldn't have separate rooms.

To hell with him, she thought. To hell with Ricky Farland. A wedding ring didn't give him the right to sleep with her after he'd crawled over half the willing flesh in North Landing.

She threw back her head and laughed. She'd driven him to it, he had said.

"I'm not a machine," he had told her one night, trying to push past her door. She had felt his eyes going down over her négligée, pulling it off her body. "Della, I'm only human! You don't know what you do to a man!"

She looked at herself in the mirror and smiled. She knew well enough what she did to men. She had known it as a young girl in Iceland, even before she had come to the States and taken that two years of school on an exchange scholarship. But she'd been even more aware of it by the time she had gone back and, if there had ever been any doubts in her mind, these had soon been dispelled by the Americans who worked at Keflavik, the big air base. She had, she felt, bargained well. Ricky had given her a beautiful home, he kept her bank account above the five thousand dollar mark, and he made love to her every chance she gave him. A girl, she supposed, could hardly ask for more.

The face that looked back at her from the mirror was not in any sense a cosmetic counter face. Della's lips were naturally full and dark and the bright red of her cheeks had been inherited from her father, an Icelander. Her sea blue eyes and soft golden hair were endowments from her mother, who had come to the island as a girl from the Danish mainland.

Her glance moved from her face down over the full, ripe lines of her body. Her breasts were high and pointed, the nipples fiery red and swollen.

"You ought to wear a brassiere," Ricky had told her once. "A guy with only half his sight can see through that blouse."

That had been during her second week in the States, almost a year before, when they had gone to a dance down at the Landing.

"I'm sorry," she had said. "I didn't realize."

After that, whenever she had gone out, she had worn a bra but she hadn't ever been able to get used to the things. She wondered, too, still looking into the mirror, how American women could get themselves into those tight little girdles. Why, she was only twenty-four inches around the middle and she'd feel like somebody was strangling her if she had to put one on. The way some women dressed they could pass themselves off for statues in a park, they were so stiffened up.

"Mrs. Farland," Jennie said from the other side of the door. "Please, Mrs. Farland, Mr. Abbott came with the eggs and he said, if I hurried, I could—"

"Oh, all right." Della's rounded hips and long, slim legs flashed in the mirror as she went to the door and jerked it open. "What is it you want?"

The girl's eyes focused on the nude figure before her and her mouth widened.

"I'd like to go to the Landing tonight," Jennie said. Her voice was desperate. "I—I have to go, Mrs. Farland."

Jennie was in her early twenties, had straight black hair—and unreadable black eyes. Her round face was always sad and worn, as if she were constantly chasing something up hill. The lines of her body, however, even under the ill-fitting green uniform, were attractive and generous.

"You've been going to town almost every night," Della reminded the girl. "When I hired you, the arrangement was for two nights off a week. Do you remember that?"

Jennie looked at the floor. "Yes, Mrs. Farland."

"That's because I don't like to be alone, Jennie. And with Mr. Farland away so much, I have to depend on you."

Tears filled Jennie's eyes.

"I know all that, Mrs. Farland. But—well, just tonight—oh, Mrs. Farland, I just have to get down to the Landing tonight! I honest have to!"

Della came out into the bedroom and closed the bath room door. She crossed to the dresser and picked up a cigarette. She knew, without looking, that Jennie's face was flushed a bright red. She always seemed to embarrass Jennie when she walked around without her clothes on. She smiled and lit the cigarette, blowing the smoke at her reflection in the mirror.

"Tell me," Della said, turning slowly. "What's your trouble, Jennie? This boy you've been seeing? This what's his name?"

"Sammy," Jennie said solemnly.

"You're in love with him?"

Jennie shook her head, her eyes dull and distant.

"Then he's in love with you?"

Jennie started to cry, silently, and nodded her head.

"I thought so," Della said, crushing the cigarette into the ashtray. She walked toward the girl. "You're going to have a baby. Is that it, Jennie? You're going to have a baby?"

For an answer the girl let out a little frightened cry and stumbled toward the door.

Della grabbed her by the shoulders, "I asked you a question."

"Let me go!" the girl pleaded. "Please!"

"You don't have to be afraid," Della said, her voice suddenly gentle. "If that's what it is, I'll help you, Jennie. I'll do everything I can."

She felt the tenseness go out of Jennie's shoulders, saw the quick smile as the girl swung around, choking against the tears.

"You will, Mrs. Farland?"

"Of course."

Jennie's eyes were huge and grateful. "You'll help me with Sammy, Mrs. Farland? You honestly will?"

"I don't know about Sammy," Della said, "I'll talk to him, if that's what you mean. But you don't have to worry about a place to stay, or your job. You can stay right here, Jennie. Just don't worry. You have to take care of yourself now, you know."

Jennie nodded and moved to the door.

"It's all right, then, if I go down to the Landing with Mr. Abbott?"

"Certainly, Jennie."

"Thank you." At the doorway the girl hesitated, looking scared again. Then, suddenly, the words came out in a rush. "You aren't what they say at all, Mrs. Farland. You aren't what I thought, either. You aren't hard and—cruel. You're good—nice. I don't care if some people do think that you're mean to Mr. Farland, I think you're—you're a lady!"

Della turned back to the mirror, smiling, listening to the pound of Jennie's heels going down the rear stairs to the kitchen. Hell, she thought, I'm no lady. I'm just an Icelander who knows how to treat people when they get into a jam. In Della's native country there were no bastards. One baby was as good as another, whether the father admitted to him or not.

It wasn't a question of being a lady. It was, in Della's opinion, simply a matter of treating trouble in the only way that it could be treated.

She sat down at the vanity table and examined her face in the mirror. She had enough of her own problems with Ricky these days, in spite of the beautiful face she saw in the mirror, and she couldn't waste all night thinking about Jennie. Besides, Ricky had called on the phone a few minutes before she'd gone into the shower, and had said that he would be home shortly, that he wanted to talk to her as soon as he got there. She wondered, idly, whether he would be drunk or sober.

The phone rang, just as she was about to slip dutifully into her brassiere—the black net thing that let the skin show through—and she answered it.

"Hi, Della," Sally Berringer breathed. "Is Ricky in yet?"

The bitch, Della thought. When would she wake up to the fact that she had lost him, that Ricky was married just as solidly as though his feet were set in concrete? Or was Sally like the rest of the girls Ricky knew, trading something that they had for anything that money could buy them? No, Della decided, Sally wouldn't be like that. Sally was a doctor's daughter, she was pretty and smart and she would only play for keeps. In a way, Della supposed, that was the thing that bothered her. Maybe Sally was still playing for keeps.

"You still there, Della?"

"Yes."

"I was asking about Ricky."

"He isn't home yet."

"Oh, darn!"

"Anything I can do?"

"Well—yes, would you give him a message? Ask him to call Roger Adams, down at the Landing, and put in a good word for me, would you? Della, I've got a terrific chance with them for a wonderful job and Ricky's word might help. I mentioned Ricky to Mr. Adams and he seems to like Ricky and—"

"All right," Della said impatiently, "I'll do it. When and if he gets home." She picked up a powder puff and ran it lazily across her jutting breasts. "I'm just surprised that you're out jobhunting, Sally. Your folks have all the money in the world. Besides, I thought you and that young fellow—the one who does advertising—might make a match of it."

"You mean Ed Loring?"

"Yes."

"Oh, heavens, he can't even support himself, Della! You know how it is with these advertising fellows; they get fifteen percent and half the time that fifteen percent is figured on nothing. So please, ask Ricky to give Mr. Adams a buzz, will you?"

"I promise."

"And maybe I'll stop around later this evening."

Don't break your back doing it, Della thought, hanging up. She guessed she could get through one Saturday night without having Sally on hand to fall all over Ricky every chance she got.

Saturday night. Saturday night at Raven's Nest on Lake Sorrow. Della went to the bedroom window and pulled aside the curtain. Slightly below and to the right of the long rolling green lawn lay the lake, its glasslike surface reflecting the red fire of the late June sun. Lake Sorrow, the natives called it now, but before, a long time ago, the Indian name for it had been the Lake of Tears.

Della sighed, closed the curtains, and went over to the bed. She sat down, stretching her long legs, looking at them. They were nice legs, smooth and tan. Lithe, soft legs meant for a man. She laughed again and patted her white stomach. She wished that her stomach and breasts weren't so white, that she could get tanned all over. In Iceland, where she had been brought up, men and women lay in the sun without any clothes on and thought nothing of it. And they went swimming, together, without wearing bathing suits. There was nothing irregular about it. It was the way they lived.

She lay back on the bed, still thinking about it. There was no prudery in Iceland, not like there was here in the States. If you didn't know what it was all about and you wanted to look, you took a look. It was like having to go to the bathroom when you were riding on a bus. In the States you gritted your teeth and hoped to God the driver wouldn't hit a hard bump. In Iceland you simply asked the driver to stop, got out, walked around in back of the bus and took care of things.

Della broke out of her reverie. She stepped into a pair of brief net panties, a half slip of the same material and then, on impulse, cast the brassiere aside. For a dress she chose a deep yellow cotton with plunging neckline, and when she finally glanced at herself in the mirror she decided that it had been a good selection. She didn't know why Ricky thought the neckline too low—all a person could see was a little of her cleft and the rising mounds on either side—but, of course, she didn't bend forward and examine the dress the way Ricky had examined it.

Saturday night, she thought again. Saturday night and she ought to go down to the kitchen and make sure that Jennie had set out the picnic stuff. But she wouldn't. She didn't give a darn. She was getting sick and tired of this every-Saturday-night rumpus.

"Nothing like eating out in the open," Ricky would say.

Indeed, Della thought, there was nothing like it. Ricky would be half drunk and he'd want to do the cooking and the hamburgers and the steaks would either fall in the fire or get wiped across the ground before they were eaten. Nobody would eat much, anyway, but they would drink a lot and maybe Ricky's sister, Gladys Anderson, would get sick on the beer and the liquor and her husband, a doctor, would say that the food had been left out in the heat and that it was spoiled.

And that Sally Berringer would show up—"I just happened to be passing"—and she'd make it her business to hang around Ricky and the fire. Of course, the road up to Raven's Nest was a dead-end affair but that didn't matter—Sally was just going by. Sometimes she brought somebody with her and they were usually real drips, except for the one fellow, that Ed Loring, and he had been all right. Dark hair and dark eyes and long and lean, he'd asked Della to dance with him. She hadn't wanted to, not really, but Ricky had been getting impossible—"I married an Icelander and I can't get her thawed out, but..." and she accepted Ed Loring's suggestion. He was a good dancer, moving easily and not holding her too close and once, when his lips had accidentally brushed her forehead, she had felt different, almost free.

"You have a beautiful command of English," he had told her. "One would never guess that you'd been born in a foreign country."

"Some day," she had said, "English will be more universal in Iceland than Danish. You see, much of the foreign trade is carried on with the

United States and there are Americans on the island all the time. Most all of us learn it and, for some reason, we are able to learn it without an accent. A few, like myself, come to the States to finish our education in one of the colleges."

Later that night, after everybody had gone, Ricky had followed her to her room.

"Let me in, doll."

"Not tonight, Ricky."

He had kicked at the locked door, sending crashing sounds all through the house.

"What the hell's the matter with you, Della?"

Silently she had undressed and crawled into bed, wishing that he wouldn't act like this,

"Damned women!" Ricky had stormed, still kicking at the door.

He'd said more, called her other names, but she hadn't listened to him. Her pillow had grown wet with tears, just as it had grown wet with her tears on other nights.

"Ricky," she had told him once, during the early days of their marriage. "Don't laugh at me, Ricky. But I'm—scared."

"Scared? What of, baby?"

"My mother's dead. And my father's dead."

"Yes."

"And there's just the two of us, Ricky. I don't have anyone else. Nobody. No one at all."

He had laughed at her then and she hadn't confided in him anymore, hadn't ever told him about how she worried over his constant drinking, or of how frightened she was to be so alone in a strange country. She had wanted to explain how important it was for her to have a baby— not someone to cling to 'her but someone she could cling to—only she hadn't been able to do a very good job of it. Every time she mentioned it to him, at first, he'd laugh at her and want to know why she wanted to ruin her swell figure getting big with a kid.

"Hell, you don't want to get yourself fixed up like that, baby. We're young and the world's brand new. Let's have fun. Kids will come later."

"Well, don't call me baby, then."

"Why not?"

"I don't like it. Save it for our real child."

"To hell with you, then. You think you're going to jump on me every time I open my mouth just because I don't see eye to eye with you on this? You're my wife, baby, and I'll call you any name I want to. You hear me? You can either like it or you can go back to Iceland and marry some fish-head eating mojack. Maybe you'd like that better, huh, baby? Maybe you'd like that better than a thirty-five-thousand-dollar house and a dame to pick up the dust after you."

That had been their first, and most serious, argument. She had been left terrified and speechless by it and when Ricky had struck her across the mouth with the flat of his hand, she had fled from their bedroom. And she had never gone back. She'd taken the room at the end of the hall, hoping it was for just one night or a week at the most.

"Okay, save it," Ricky told her one evening. "You think you're any different from the rest of the dames? You think a guy can't relax with some classy company whenever he feels like it?"

"I'm sorry, Ricky. Forgive me."

She had let him into her room that night and afterward she had felt worse than a common prostitute. He'd been drinking heavily and had said things to her that no man had ever said before. Later, she had heard him sick in the bathroom and then she had been sick and she hadn't let him into her room again for a month.

It had gotten worse, she thought now, much worse. Sometimes she wished that Ricky's father hadn't left him all that money, that Ricky had to go out to work and earn a living. The seemingly limitless funds bought new cars and fine clothes and even finer women. Some times, when Ricky was staying away overnight, either at the Landing or at Port Jervis, he would call her on the phone and in the background she would hear a girl's laughter. Mocking laughter. Laughter for Ricky—at a price.

She walked around her bedroom, thinking about it. Things couldn't go on this way, not forever. They had to end sometime, somewhere, somehow. It wasn't a matter of love anymore; it was a matter of survival.

Either Ricky would destroy her.

Or she would destroy Ricky.

It was as simple as that.

2

SHE HEARD RICKY drive up at about seven and park the long green Caddy in the rear of the house. The sounds of a man's muffled curse and a woman's high-pitched laughter came through the open window. Della sighed and stretched out luxuriously on the wide, soft bed. Her luck was getting worse all the time; Ricky's sister and brother-in-law had driven out with him.

The kitchen screendoor slammed, and after a few moments, she heard Ricky coming up the stairs.

"Hey!" he yelled. "Where's Jennie?"

"She went down to the Landing."

"Not a thing is ready," he complained. "How come?"

"I don't know," Della told him. "Jennie must have forgotten."

Ricky came and stood in the doorway. He had a long, powerful body with narrow waist and wide shoulders. He grinned at her and pushed his tousled brown hair back from his forehead.

"The dutiful housewife," Ricky observed. "Flat on her back on the bed."

Della sat up.

"Let's not fight," Della suggested. "Let's try to be human beings for one night."

"Sure."

He came into the room, still looking at her.

"Human beings," he said. "That's for me."

He moved fast, grabbing her by the arm. He pushed the arm behind her, twisting it and she arched her back. He held her that way, smiling down into her face.

"You've got a good idea, baby. Let's get human."

She tried to pull free but he held her fast.

"You ape," she told him. "Let me go!"

He shook his head.

"I said I wanted to talk to you, didn't I? Well, this is what I want to tell you. I'm getting out of here tomorrow." He paused and then laughed as bewilderment filled her eyes. "Oh, it's just for a week, baby, just for a week."

She wished that he would take his hands from her.

"I see," she said.

"Don't you want to know where I'm going?" His lips brushed her mouth. "Or don't you give a damn?"

"If you care to tell me."

"Fishing." He increased the pressure on her arm and she bent further backward over the bed. "Up to Roscoe, on the Beaverkill. Best trout stream in the world. I'm going to take a room, forget about the booze and fish for a week."

His free hand went to her hair, grabbed it and jerked her head back. "Kiss me, baby."

She tried to shake her head free but her scalp felt as though a thousand hot needles were being shoved into it.

"You don't have to hurt me, Ricky," she whispered. "You don't have to do that."

He let go of her hair and cradled the back of her head in the palm of his hand. "All you have to do is show a little wifely affection and you won't have any trouble at all."

She felt her head being driven forward and then his mouth was down there on her lips, wet and wide; his tongue slamming up against her teeth. He released her arm and his hand went down to the small of her back, crushing her up against him.

"You've been driving me nuts," he breathed.

She struggled for a moment and then stopped. He was too strong for her.

"You don't have to force a kiss," Della said. "You could ask me nicely."

"And have you tell me to go to hell?"

"Try it."

"All right." He released her, standing there with his face flushed and perspiring. "So I'm asking, baby. A nice long sweet kiss."

"Your sister's waiting downstairs."

"The hell with her," Ricky said. "So what if she and that jerky husband of hers are waiting? They aren't going anywhere and they've got all night to get there."

She jumped up and attempted to run around him, to get away, but again he caught her.

"You haven't got the guts to say it, baby."

He shoved her down on the bed, holding her there. She kicked at him. His eyes were cloudy and wild.

"You're my wife," he said.

The tears were in her voice. "Don't, Ricky!"

She closed her eyes, not wanting to look at him, not wanting to see him, hoping that the humiliation of this moment would die in the darkness.

He swore at her and jerked savagely at the yellow dress, ripping it from top to bottom. Her flesh spilled into the open, heaving.

'T'll give you credit," Ricky told her. "You sure are stacked."

"I hate you," Della said miserably. "I hate you, Ricky Farland."

His mouth covered her lips. "Kiss me, baby! Kiss Me!"

She lay beneath him on the bed, her lips unresponsive, her body limp. Bitterly she endured the desires of her husband.

Later she reached up and shoved his head away.

"You've had your fun," she said in disgust. "Get up."

"I never worked so hard in my life," Ricky sighed.

Della walked to the dresser and stood there watching him in the mirror.

"I hate you," she said and picked up the comb.

"You'll hate me more when I get back," he assured her. "I'm going to have news for you, baby."

She tossed her blonde head contemptuously.

"See you downstairs," Ricky said and left the room.

She went over to the closet and got into another cotton dress, a crisp white one. She glanced into the mirror again, decided that her hair was passable, and followed Ricky downstairs.

"Hell of a note," he greeted her in the kitchen. "Nothing ready."

She got the hamburger out of the refrigerator and dropped it into the basket. Next, she took the buns from the cabinet and the silverware from one of the drawers and put these in with the hamburgers.

"You can bring the butter and the booze," she told him, picking up the basket.

She started for the door and he stepped in front of her.

"Look," he said. "About what just happened—"

"You got what you were after," she reminded him coldly. "Let's skip it."

She walked past him and out of the house. The smoke from the charcoal fire filled the air and the night was clear and hot. She went around the building and over toward the fireplace.

Damn Ricky, she thought, why did he have to go and do a thing like that?

Damn him, she'd make him pay. Some day he'd pay big for taking her that way and making her feel like a two-dollar whore...

"Hi,' Gladys Anderson said. "What kept you so long?"

"I was flat on my back," Della replied, putting the basket on the table.

Ricky's sister was a tall girl with a thin face and an unimportant body. Her one claim to beauty was a dimple in the middle of her chin.

"It's hot enough to put anybody on his back," Doctor Anderson said, straightening up from the fire.

Paul Anderson looked something like his wife, tall and thinfaced, and bent in a slight stoop.

"God," Gladys sighed, looking into the basket. "Hamburgers. Why doesn't somebody invent something else to eat?"

"There's steak inside," Della said. "And pork chops. But you'll have to help yourself. Jennie's out."

"I wouldn't want to eat pork fixed this way," Paul Anderson said. "You know, if pork isn't cooked enough, why—"

"Oh, shut up," his wife said, without feeling. She looked toward the house. "Where are Ricky and the drinks? God Almighty, it's a good thing he doesn't have to earn a living waiting on tables."

Paul Anderson scowled at his wife.

"I wish you wouldn't talk like that," he said. "I don't know what's got into you these days, Gladys."

His wife wheeled on him angrily.

"Well, I'll tell you what's the matter with me," she stormed. "You want to know, so I'll tell you."

"Gladys!"

"You know where I was all afternoon?"

"Playing bridge," her husband said lamely,

"And with whom?"

"The Choir Club."

"That's right," Gladys sneered. "The Choir Club. A bunch of phonies if I ever saw any. And you know why? Well, I'll tell you why. Because you wanted me to. Because you said I should go to affairs like that so those old rips will come to you when they get a pain in their can. And another thing—"

"Gladys!"

"Don't you Gladys me!" she yelled. "I'm getting sick of it, do you hear? Just because you think it isn't right to live off my money and you want to be a lousy doctor, that's no reason for me to spend half my life playing stick-in-the-mud with a bunch of old bags!"

"All right, Gladys." Her husband turned away, went over to the fire and stirred it. "Forget it. I'm sorry I imposed on you."

"Old bags!" Gladys insisted. "The only thing any of them are suffering from is lack of brains."

Della placed the silverware on the table but left the rolls covered. A fly stabbed unhappily at the cellophane.

"Did I hear sounds of a rumpus?" Ricky wanted to know, arriving with a tub of ice packed around cans of beer. Hamburgers rested precariously on top of the ice. "Sounded like the fighting Andersons to me."

"It was," Paul Anderson admitted. He grinned at his wife. "She won again."

"Well, don't hold anything back," Ricky said, placing the tub on the end of the table. "You can scream all you want to out here and nobody'll bother you."

"The night isn't over," his sister said, opening a can of beer. She lifted it and drank slowly. "Golly, that's good!" She slapped her brother on the arm. "Knock me out, kid."

Ricky punched a hole in a can and held it aloft.

"To the drunken Farlands," he proclaimed. "Long may they stagger."

Della made up the hamburgers and placed them on the rack. The others sat on the ground near the fire and the doctor was starting on his second can of beer. After a while they would eat and then they would drink some more—either beer or liquor from the house—and by midnight the place would be a mess.

"Oh, I must tell you," Della remembered suddenly. "Sally phoned, Ricky. Wanted you to call a Mr. Adams about some job she's trying to get."

"That idiot," Ricky said, getting up. "There's only one kind of a job he'd want to give her."

The doctor, now mellowed by the beer, snickered.

"As who wouldn't?" he wanted to know.

"Men," Gladys said, glancing at Della. "They've all got their minds between their legs."

"I'll call her," Ricky said, starting for the house. "Be right back."

"That must be why you call me feebleminded," the doctor said to his wife.

"Oh, shut up," Gladys told him dispassionately.

The night shadows slid in across the lake and in the distance a loon cried. From the direction of Port Jervis could be heard the sounds of an Erie freight train hammering its way up the mountain.

"Beer's nice and' cold," Della said, opening a can.

"Never saw you drink much," Paul Anderson observed.

Della smiled.

"I can't. Icelanders are like the American Indian when it comes to drinking. We just go wild."

The doctor leaned forward, squinting.

"How wild?" he wanted to know.

They all laughed.

Ricky, returning, opened a can of beer and sat down next to Paul Anderson.

Della took a long drink of her beer.

"Sally's coming up later," Ricky said. "With that Loring fellow. 'Hell,' I said to her, 'I don't know why you want to go and get a job—you have plenty of money. You know what she said to me? She said, 'I have to get a job because I can't find anything to do any other way. Isn't that rich?'"

Anderson said, "I wish I had just half her old man's practice, that's what I wish."

"So do I," his wife agreed.

"Well, I guess it takes a while to get one built up," Anderson said. "A guy has to keep plugging year after year."

"We might as well eat," Della said. "No point in waiting for Sally."

"You know it," Anderson said. "That Loring fellow looked like a bush man to me. Those two may never get here."

"Not Sally," Ricky said. "She's not that kind."

"Well, you ought to know," his sister said. "You were engaged to her once and you probably made enough tries at it."

They sat down at the table and pawed through the food. Just as they were finishing a car drove in, its headlights washing across them.

"Where's this Loring from?" Gladys asked.

"Nobody knows," Ricky told her.

"Very, very funny, brother."

The man who came toward them was tall and dark and he had lean hips. Della could remember the hard feel of his body, the sure touch of his hands. She wondered, rather hopefully, if he might want to dance again.

"Hello, you nice people," Ed Loring said.

The girl with him was short and dark and wore white shorts in decided contrast to her browned legs. Her white halter was amply filled.

"Hello," she said. She had a pleasant voice, smooth and soft, and Della was forced to admit that Sally Berringer also had more than her share of poise. "Ricky," she said, turning her attention to him. "You've got me all upset, hon. What's this you say about Mr. Adams?"

"He's a wolf."

"Ricky, he's old enough to be my father!"

"Then he's an old wolf."

"I don't believe it." Then, to Ed Loring, "A tall, cool one, Ed."

"Coming up." The ice rattled in the tub. "How about you, Mrs. Farland?"

"Well—all right."

She seldom drank anything but Ricky was going to be away for a week and she felt relieved about that. She'd been wanting to have Helga Johnsdottir up from Newark for a few days and this might be a good opportunity. She hadn't invited Helga while Ricky was home because Ricky would only insult her about Iceland and Helga wasn't a girl to kid around with very much.

"Well, who wants to work, anyway?" Sally was saying. "So I won't get my Social Security when I'm sixty-five."

Anderson opened several cans of beer, passing them around.

"Hey, Della," Ricky said. "You're gonna get crocked like you never got crocked before."

"No, I won't."

"She's celebrating my departure," Ricky told everybody. "Maybe she's got a lover who'll take my place." "Or a lover who already took it," Sally suggested.

There was a moment's silence, broken only by the peepers along the lake.

"I'll read you a letter from home," Della told her slowly. "That's the first crack you ever made like that and it had better be the last. In case you'd like to know, this socalled iceberg has plenty of fire inside."

Somebody laughed but she couldn't tell who. She thought it might be Ed Loring. And she thought, too, though she couldn't be sure of it, that Loring's eyes had hardly left her since his arrival.

"I've just been briefed on a very important point," Ricky said. "My wife has a temper."

Gladys pushed her beer can aside and tactfully stood up. "Hell, it's hot!" she said. "Who's for swimming?"

"You just ate," Ricky reminded her. "You're supposed to drink all the beer and relax for an hour. Ask the doc."

"You'll die when your time comes, not before," Anderson said, joining his wife. "Besides, water is the cheapest way of doing away with yourself. There are no expenses."

"A gruesome bunch," Sally Berringer stated. "But I'll join you, anyway. Can I swim in my shorts?"

"You can swim in nothing," Ricky said. He glanced at Della. "That's the way they do it in Iceland, isn't it?"

"Quite often."

"You ever?" Anderson wanted to know.

"Of course."

"With men?"

"Men and women."

"I'm taking the next plane out," swore Anderson.

"You coming, Della?" asked Ricky. "Or staying?"

"Staying."

"Loring?"

"Not me," Ed Loring said. "I wouldn't swim in the dark if you paid me diver's wages."

"Well, then, that leaves you, Sally," Ricky said. "You won't let me down, will you?"

Della saw her hand find Ricky's in the shadows.

"I'll never let you down," she said. "And you know it."

After they had gone, Della began cleaning up the table. Loring stood nearby, watching her.

"Here, let me help," he said as. she reached for the tub.

"They'll want more," Della told him. "I was just going to fill it."

"Some crew," Loring observed as they walked toward the house.

"Yes."

"I didn't mean anything disrespectful."

"No. But they are a wild bunch."

"The Berringer girl seems pretty steady."

They entered the kitchen and Della flipped on the light. Della put the silverware in the sink and then showed Loring where the icemaking machine was, over in the corner past the deep freeze unit. The muscles on Loring's arm rippled as he scooped out the ice and filled the tub.

"We won't bother with the beer," Della told him. "That's down in the cellar and Ricky'll have to get it. Probably they won't want any more beer, anyway."

"Liquor?"

She nodded.

"I don't know how you stand it," he said.

They went back outside, returning to the picnic area. Loring put the tub of ice on the end of the table and lit a cigarette.

"There's a couple of cold cans left. Want one?"

She felt unusually hot, the night closing in around her. She guessed it was the beer, because beer always made her feel this way, hot and lazy.

"All right," Della said. "No sense letting it go to waste."

"You know, you speak our language very well, Mrs. Farland."

"I'd rather you called me Della."

"Okay. Della."

"I had two years of college in the States," she explained, inhaling the smoke. "I won it in school, in a contest. And, of course, English is taught in the schools in Iceland. Then, too, there were many soldiers and civilians stationed at the airport at Keflavik. You couldn't help learning it."

"That's where you met your husband?"

"Yes."

She took her beer over to the glider swing and sat down. It was her favorite spot to sit in the evening because she could watch the moon coming up over the lake and she could listen to the noises of the night all around her.

"Mind if I join you?" Loring sat down beside her and the springs sagged. "Sounds like they're having quite a ball down there," he said.

Shouts and laughter floated up from the lake, followed by a tremendous splash.

"One thing," Della said, "they're all very good swimmers."

They sat silently for a few moments, smoking and drinking their beer. She felt Loring's arm close to her, brushing against her every time he lifted the can to his mouth.

"Iceland must be quite a place," he said finally. "I've never been there but I've read about it. Was your husband in the service when you met him?"

"No. He came up there with his father's construction company but the job was called off."

She remembered the first time she had met Ricky, in front of the Massey Mess Hall at the airport. He had been standing in the rain, dripping wet, and he asked her about the bus schedule to the hotel. She told him that a bus ought to be along almost any minute and, since she was also waiting for transportation to the hotel, they stood there talking. He explained that he'd just arrived from the States the night before, that the food was better than he had expected and that Iceland boasted the wettest rains of any place he'd ever been in. Finally, when the bus appeared, Ricky tried to get on it from the wrong side—in Iceland you boarded a bus from the left side—and they sat together and laughed about it all the way to the hotel...

"What kind of work does your husband do now, Della?"

She hated to tell him. She always hated to answer that question. Nothing, that's what Ricky did, absolutely nothing. His father died shortly before his return to the States, leaving half of his cash and all of his construction company to Ricky. Della could still recall the tears in the eyes of the men who had served the company so long and so well when Ricky had informed them that he didn't plan to continue.

"He doesn't do anything," she replied. "Ricky is—retired."

Ed Loring whistled and leaned back.

"Boy!" he exclaimed. "It must be great to have that kind of money."

Della didn't know how much money her husband had. Once, in Iceland he had talked about half a million dollars but that had been the night they had visited his hut and he had been drinking. That had also been the night when she had made it very clear to Ricky that he would never know what she was like until he put a wedding band on her finger. For a long time after that she had thought Ricky was in love with her but now, slightly more than a year later, she felt that he had only been lonely.

"Money isn't everything," Della told Ed Loring. "You have to have some of it, but it isn't—everything."

"You sound depressed."

"Maybe I am."

"Don't mind me," he said. "I ask too damned many questions. But I'm new here and I'm trying to find my way around."

"Oh. I thought you were a native. I don't know why, but I did."

"I'm from upper New York. My sister went to college with Sally and that's how come I'm tied up with her. Nothing serious. She's just showing me around."

Della laughed and fell back against the cushions. She had been right about the beer. It made her feel hot and lazy and completely relaxed.

"And here I was thinking this was a big romance," she murmured. "How wrong can I be?"

Ed Loring smiled and tossed his cigarette into the grass.

"Look," he said, moving closer to Della. "I might as well be honest about it. I came to North Landing for just one purpose. Do you know what it is?"

"No."

"Well, I've been here about. two weeks. Sally has been nice enough to drag me over half the countryside, introduce me to a lot of people. I think I now know enough about North Landing and Port Jervis and the rest of this area to make my move and either close a deal with someone' or catch the next train out."

"I'm sorry," Della said. "I don't follow you."

"You wouldn't be expected to." Ed Loring's face came closer. She could see his slow smile and his white teeth. She could also feel his arm slide gently down across her shoulders. "But of all of the people I have met here, Della, you're the only one who looks like a prospect."

"Prospect?"

"Yes."

"Please," she said, trying to move away from his arm. "My husband will be back soon."

"Not from the sounds from down there, he won't." Laughter and whistles and shouts filled the night and Ed Loring's arm tightened. "Look," he went on quickly, "you're a beautiful girl and all that, but I'm not here looking for romance. I'm a businessman trying to find someone who has a select location—very private, like yours—and who happens to be interested in picking up a little money."

She relaxed, staring at him. She didn't know whether to feel glad or sorry about his claim that his approach wasn't a personal one. There was something about the admiration of a handsome man that any girl liked, married or not.

"I don't need any money," she told Ed Loring.

"We'll talk about that later."

"All right." She thought about the balance in her checking account and she wanted to laugh. She did.

"It isn't very funny."

"My apology, Mr. Loring."

"Call me Ed."

"All right, Ed."

"You're from Iceland." His voice was now very earnest. "Right?"

"Right."

"And some of your customs up there are different from ours?"

"Some of them, yes."

"Take men and women, for instance. They go swimming together up there and they don't wear any suits. Am I correct?"

"In some of the pools they don't. In some they do."

He was quiet for a moment.

"Have you ever gone in swimming where they wore no suits?"

"Of course."

"And did you feel ashamed?"

"About what?" '

His eyes moved over her, smiling.

"That was a silly question. You haven't got anything to be ashamed of. What I meant is, did you think it wrong?"

"Not if people wanted to do it."

His head was closer now.

"Not if they wanted to do it in Iceland—or here?"

Della smiled at him.

"Well, I'm not going to take off my clothes and go swimming with you—Ed."

"Oh, hell!" He sounded almost angry. "I didn't mean that. I'm just talking in general terms, See, some people want to do things like that in the States. Not just swimming. They believe in going nude for their health. Know what I'm driving at?"

She nodded. In Iceland great stress was laid upon the value of the rays of the sun. She remembered her father telling her, as a child, how the Icelanders had, in times gone by, begun the process of drying cod in the sun. At the start, it had not been because the fish could be cured that way but due to the belief that some of the health giving emanations of the sun would be captured and imprisoned in the flesh.

"There's a lot of good in the sun," Della admitted. "Several months out of the year, we'd hardly ever see the sun in Iceland. There's a great deal of tuberculosis there and very few Icelanders have good teeth. And an American up there—well, if an American cuts himself, no matter how slightly, it usually takes weeks and weeks for him to heal. I've heard it's because of the lack of sun."

"There's no doubt about it," Ed assured her. "And another thing—how many—well, sex crimes do you have in Iceland?"

Della told him that she couldn't remember a single one committed by an Icelandic male. There had been two, however, involving Americans from the airbase.

"Right. And there is also the matter of juvenile delinquency," he said. "There is hardly any record of delinquency or sex crime among people who practice nudism."

"Nudism?"

"Yes." He took his arm away from her, fumbled for another cigarette and offered her one. The match came to life and they both lit up at the same time. "I might just as well be frank about it, Della. I'm not an advertising man. I said I was but only because that seemed to be the best way to get Sally to take me around. Actually, I'm employed by a nudist camp in South Jersey, a camp that wants to move farther north. There are several places around my home, in upper New York, but they wouldn't be any good. Al Smith saw to that."

"Who is Al Smith?"

"He used to be governor of New. York. It was during his time that they passed a law outlawing nudism with in the state."

"That doesn't seem very fair. As long as people keep to themselves and don't bother others, I don't see what's wrong with it."

"I'm glad to hear you talk like that," Ed said.

"Well, that's the way I feel about it."

"But some legislators don't. However here in New Jersey it's okay to operate a nudist camp, though you have to be careful about it. You have to be sure that you don't annoy other people. That's why it's so hard to find a place in which to locate. Also, there are a lot of good spots that won't let you in; either the people who own the land think you're crazy or they're afraid of what the neighbors will say."

The sounds from the lake were beginning to diminish. Della could hear Ricky's loud voice, calling to someone, followed by Sally's low, musical laughter.

"And you think I wouldn't care, is that it?" she wanted to know. "You think it wouldn't bother me if people ran all over the place without any clothes on. And you think I wouldn't care what the neighbors said? Is that why you're talking to me about it?"

Ed Loring was silent for a long moment.

"I guess you could say that. Yes."

"And what about my husband?"

Ed shrugged, did not answer.

"What about my husband?" she persisted. "What do you think he would say? Unless there were lots of pretty girls and he had a chance to chase every one of them? What do you think he would say about this?"

"Believe something," Ed Loring told her slowly. "Believe me when I tell you that in all my twenty-five years of living I have never carried tales. I don't intend to start now, Della. All I'll say is that your husband won't enter into it. I indicated before that I thought you would be able to use the money. I'm sure you will. But I'm not going into that now. That is something for an other time. All I wanted to do tonight is tell you about what I have in mind and ask that you think about it. If it should fit in with your plans, all right. If it doesn't, that's all right, too."

Something gripped her down inside, deep and cold. Money. She had never thought of it much before. Being married to Ricky had made it unnecessary to think about money.

"I don't know what you're trying to say," Della whispered unevenly. "I don't know what you're trying to tell me."

"I think you do."

Her eyes sought his in the darkness,

"Please, tell me. I want to know."

"It wouldn't be right."

"It would be fair."

His arm tightened across her shoulders, bringing her closer.

"Another thing you have to believe," he said. "I didn't come here for—for intimacies, But you're very beautiful, Della. You know that. Men have told you that before. Your husband must have told you that many, many times. But I haven't. Not until now. And I want to. I want to tell you that I think you're the most beautiful girl I've ever seen."

"I wish you wouldn't say things like that."

His free hand found her chin, tilting her face. His lips were very close and she could smell the clean odor of shaving lotion.

"I'm not going to kiss you," he said. "I'm not going to paw you. I'm just going to tell you a couple of things for sure, Della. A couple of things that have nothing to do with business."

She tried to say something, but she was all choked up inside. Her breath was coming deeply and irregularly and she could feel her breasts, hard and full, pushing out against him. She wanted to cry out, to break away from him, but she couldn't. He had walked toward her out of the night just a short time before and now she wanted to cling to him, to hold him close, because he was all that seemed to be real. It was a crazy, terrible, wonderful feeling.

"I'm no prince," Ed Loring told her, his clean breath washing across her face. "And I've got no money. But I know what I like. I like you, Della. You're different.I don't know how the hell you got mixed up with a crowd like this."

She said nothing. Her fingers touched his hair and moved away. It was too long a story. And it didn't concern Ed Loring.

"People do terrible things sometimes," Ed told her. "Other people can do it to almost any of us any time. I've had them do it to me. I've felt hurt, beaten. But I got over it. There's always something else, somebody else, somewhere to turn. Don't forget that, Della. And you can count on me. You can turn to me."

She nodded, not knowing what to say.

"You hardly know me," he went on. His lips brushed against her cheek and moved off. "And I hardly know you. But this you can be certain of—this camp thing I spoke to you about is a real opportunity. Nudism is a big movement and the people in it are willing to pay top money. If you ever need a dollar, it could be one way of turning it." If she ever needed a dollar? The coldness possessed her again, burning with the pain of fire. Ed Loring knew something that he wasn't telling her. Was it about Ricky? Was it about herself? Or both of them?

"Ed," she whispered. "Ed, please tell me whatever it is that you know!"

He hesitated an instant and then moved away from her.

"They're coming up from the lake," he said. His glance moved down across her face, swept across the jutting shelf of her breasts and back to her face again.

"I'll call you on the phone."

She thought about Ricky and the fact that he would be away all the next week. She thought, too, about how she had never looked at another man, never thought of another man, since her wedding day. She thought of some of the names Ricky had called her and that night in her bedroom when he had made her sick. She thought of the phone calls and the laughter of drunken women. She thought of these things, and of something else, too. She was so alone, so very much alone, and she was so utterly frightened. There was no one she could talk to, no one who would listen, really. Except this stranger, maybe. Except Ed...

"Please do that," she said, her voice husky. "Call me soon, Ed."

In silence they walked back to the fireplace, waiting for the others to come up from the lake.

3

IT WAS VERY early in the morning when Ricky started banging on her bedroom door. Della sat up, blinking into the sun, and stretched lazily.

"Go away," she told him.

His foot banged against the door several times.

"Hell, I'm not after what you think," he told her. "I'm looking for my camera."

"It isn't in here."

There was a moment's silence.

"I've got to talk to you, baby. Just for a couple of minutes."

She rolled over, closing her eyes.

"Don't bother me," she said, remembering last night, hating it and hating him. "Go away," she repeated.

"I am." Ricky's laughter filled the house, drifted away. "Hell, I've been up packing all night. You're damned right I'm going away. And not just for a week. For good! You hear me? For good! That's why I have to talk to you, baby."

For good? Della laughed. That would be too good to be true.

She crawled from the bed and reached for her négligée. The rays of the sun washed over her pink and white skin, caressed her hair. Shrugging into the nylon garment she crossed to the door.

"Come in," she said, unlocking it.

Ricky entered the room. She was surprised to see that he was clean-shaven and appeared quite sober. His faded khaki pants and shirt were rumpled but that wasn't unusual; he seldom worried about his appearance.

"I'm getting out of here right now," he told her, walking over to the window. "The car's packed and I'm ready. To hell with you, baby. I'm never coming back!"

"You don't have to shout."

"So who's going to hear me? There's nobody here, not even Jennie. She must have found what she needed last night."

Della's eyes flashed.

"That's an awful thing to say, Ricky."

"Yeah?" He came across the room toward her. "Hell, just the other day she comes to me and wants to borrow two hundred bucks. Can you imagine that? Some guy gives it to her good and she wants money from me."

"You didn't come in here to talk about Jennie."

"No." He lit a cigarette and watched her through the smoke. "About us. I want a divorce, baby."

She nodded. She felt no surprise whatever. They'd been running straight into it right from the start, like two trains on one track.

"Gosh, I've gone through a lot of money!" he exclaimed unexpectedly. There was dark concern in his eyes, "You've got no idea, baby. No idea."

"I never asked you to spend," she reminded him.

"You can have the place out here and the money you've got in the bank," he said, ignoring her remark. "But that's all you get, baby. That's all that's left."

"I'm sorry," Della said. She meant it. And now she was feeling surprised enough. She had thought that Ricky, if nothing else, was quite well off.

Ricky laughed.

"Don't worry about me. I'll make out all right. I'm going into business in town—lumber or hardware. Nothing sensational, but pretty solid."

Della waited a long moment before she said it.

"It's Sally, isn't it?"

He grinned.

"Sure."

"The poor damned fool," Della said. "She's got a surprise waiting for her."

"Stop feeling sorry for us."

I'm not," Della assured him. "I'm just saying."

"Well, stop saying." His eyes moved over her body, opening the négligée, closing it again. "You played me for a sucker, baby. A big one, hell, you just wanted to get to the States. Isn't that why you married me?"

"You lie!" she flung at him angrily. "I loved you, I thought you loved me."

"You just wanted a way to go stateside," he insisted. "I paid high for you, baby. But after we got here, you backed down. You wouldn't stick by the bargain."

"Because you always came to me drunk. You reviled me and—and forced me. You—"

He turned and walked to the door.

"So there's nothing more to be said. If it's okay about the divorce, I'll get in touch with Tom Fielding. He's the. lawyer."

"What can I say?" she wanted to know. "What more can either of us say that could possibly do any good?"

"Then, I'll call Fielding?"

"Yes!"

At the door Ricky paused, not looking back.

"*Guindine*, baby."

It was a word that meant "goodbye" in Icelandic.

And then he was gone and there was just the sound of his receding footsteps on the stairs to remind her that Ricky Farland had been her husband and had lived here in this house with her. Slowly she went over to the window and stood there looking out. She watched him get into the green Caddy, noted the piles of luggage in the back, and waved to him as he drove around the house. But he wasn't looking up and he didn't see her and in a couple of seconds he was gone out of sight.

She returned to the bed and looked at the clock. Five minutes before eight. What an awful time of the day, she thought, to break up a marriage. She flung herself down upon the bed, laughing. Her only feeling was one of relief.

It had been a useless, unfortunate, silly marriage. It hadn't even paid to waste all that nice paper on the certificate. They might better have played house for a year and then called the whole thing off. Or had a trial marriage, the way couples often did in Iceland.

The sun burned across her back and she rolled over into the shadows, fighting against sudden tears. Maybe it had been easy enough, while he had been here with her, to accept the fact that their union was actually ending, but now that he was gone, now that she knew that he was never coming back, she felt unaccountably desolate and lost.

Lying there on the bed she cried herself to sleep. Not until Jennie came in, shortly before noon, did she awaken.

"You sick, Mrs. Farland?" Jennie asked.

"No. I'm all right."

"I'm sorry about being late," Jennie said. "I'll make up the time, Mrs. Farland."

"Don't worry about it." She watched the girl go over and fix the curtains, closing them. The room was filled with a soft, yellow glow. "Tell me something, Jennie. What did your young man say?"

"He said—"

"You don't have to tell me if you don't want to. Perhaps I shouldn't have asked you."

"That's all right, Mrs. Farland. I'm glad you did. Before—well, before I didn't have anybody to talk to, except Sammy, and Sammy kept getting mad all the time."

"I'm happy that you got things straightened out," Della said. "When are you going to get married?"

The girl had been busy tucking the sheet in under the mattress but now she stopped, looking up.

"Gee, I'm not going to get married, Mrs. Farland. At first I was—even up to last night I was, because Sammy said it was the thing to do—but now—now that Sammy says he'll arrange things, why everything's going to be all right."

"I don't understand you, Jennie."

The girl tucked the sheet in place and patted the bed.

"Sammy's going to drive me to a doctor, Mrs. Farland. Next week. All I have to do is stay overnight and then maybe take a couple of days off. But you won't have to pay me for the time I'm off," Jennie hastened to add. "Of course, I could use the money, same as always, but I wouldn't expect you to pay me. After all—"

"Jennie!"

The girl jumped at the sharpness in Della's voice.

"It's the only thing to do," she said. "I've thought it over and over and there ain't any other way. Gee, Mrs. Farland, I'm not even twenty yet and Sammy hasn't got a very good job."

"But it's a big risk."

"Not as big as if I have the baby and can't take care of it."

"Well, I never heard of such a thing!" Della said, deeply disappointed in Jennie. "Of course you could take care of it. And that fellow of yours—that Sammy—what kind of a man is he to let you do a thing like that?"

Jennie resumed her bedmaking, saying nothing.

"You're lucky you're not going to marry a man like that. A man who would let you do away with his own child isn't much of a man at all, why, you'd think—"

"Don't you say anything about Sammy!" Jennie flared. "He's a very good boy. Gee, Mrs. Farland, Sammy loves me and he isn't that kind of a fellow at all. He's just a hard worker and he wants to do what's right."

"He certainly has a funny way of showing it," Della observed.

Jennie looked embarrassed.

"I'm sorry I got mad, Mrs. Farland. It's only that—"

"Forget it, Jennie. No harm done."

It would be another of those hot June days outside, Della thought, selecting red shorts and a white halter. The shorts were short indeed, cutting high across her full thighs, and the halter was so tight that she had to exhale before she could fasten it. Sex magnets, Ricky had described the garments. Designed to drive a man out of his mind.

"Mr. Farland told me about the two hundred dollars," Della said casually, "I'm glad you spoke to him about it."

"That's a relief," Jennie sighed. "I thought you'd be mad."

"Why should I be? After all, Mr. Farland does pretty much as he pleases." A thought, or rather a suspicion, suddenly came to her. She tried to gauge her next words carefully, cunningly. "I just hope that this trouble with Mr. Farland won't ruin things for you with your Sammy."

"Trouble? What trouble?"

"Oh, come on. You can tell me. Mr. Farland is the father, isn't he?"

Jennie said nothing. But her eyes narrowed. She seemed to be thinking hard, and into her face came a somewhat crafty look.

"Well, isn't he?" Della insisted. "Isn't that why he gave you two hundred dollars?"

"If you say so, Mrs. Farland." Jennie hesitated, then blurted, "Oh, he was awful nice about it, when I told him. At first, I thought of coming to you, but I used to hear the two of you fighting and—well, it seemed only sense that I go to Mr. Farland. He said he didn't want you to know, not at all, and that I'd done just what I should. But I guess he must have thought it over and figured it best to tell you. Anyway, I'm glad he did; I wouldn't have known how to say anything to you about it, Mrs. Farland. I honest wouldn't."

The poor, stupid little bitch, Della thought, walking over to the girl.

"Mr. Farland didn't tell me, Jennie. I just guessed it. You see, Mr. Farland left me this morning. And he isnt coming back. We're getting a divorce."

Jennie shrank back until her knees caught the edge of the bed.

"Oh, gosh, I'm always talking too much, Mrs. Farland!"

"Or doing something else too much," Della suggested.

Jennie's face burned bright red and she sank down on the bed.

"It wasn't anybody's fault, Mrs. Farland. Really, it just happened."

"I don't want to hear any more about it, Jennie." Della pulled the girl upright. "And you aren't going to do away with that child, you hear? You're going to stay right here in this house and have the baby just as God meant you to."

Tears streamed down Jennie's face.

"I'm scared," she whimpered. "Scared."

"You've got no reason to be."

"But I don't know what I'm going to do, Mrs. Farland! I'm just a kid myself. I get so worried. Honest, I do. I wake up in the night and I get scared all over, because I know nobody will want me, or give me a job afterward, and everybody will say I'm no good—"

Della grabbed the sobbing girl by the shoulders.

"You listen to me," Della told her, shaking her.

Jennie lifted her tear-filled eyes.

"Yes, Mrs. Farland."

"This is a terrible thing, Jennie, an awful thing that Ricky has done. But I don't want you to worry about the baby. There's nothing to worry about. You'll be here with me and I'll take care of you. Then, after the baby comes, if you see that you can't get along, I'll take the baby and take care of it for you. I'll take care of it for a day or a week or forever. You know what I'm saying, Jennie?"

"You're mighty good to me," Jennie said haltingly.

Della went to the dresser and impatiently lit a cigarette. "I'll tell you something about your Mr. Farland, Jennie. You want to hear something?"

Jennie looked doubtful.

"All right," she said.

"Well, I'll tell you something, Jennie. I'm mad. I'm so mad that I could kill that man. The things he's done to me, slamming me around, sleeping with every damned woman who would have him, drinking everything he could get his hands on. And then, because the rest isn't enough, he gets you pregnant and walks off and leaves me."

"Yes, Mrs. Farland."

Della felt the rage boiling within her. "You're going to have that baby, Jennie. You're going to have it if I have to crawl in bed with you and nurse it until it's old enough to go to school. And all this time that traitor of a husband of mine is going to pay and pay and pay—and pay until he's so sick of paying that he'll get down on his knees and pray that God will strike him dead!"

"Please, Mrs. Farland!" Jennie ran toward the door, frightened. "I'll do like you say, but please—"

"I'll ruin him!" Della promised herself, jerking a lamp from the night table. Jennie screamed as the lamp crashed to the floor. "The dirty, evil man!"

Jennie ran from the room, whimpering, and Della, suddenly ashamed at her display of temper, sank to the bed.

God, she thought wildly, why did Ricky have to go and do a thing like that? Hadn't he done enough already? Where was it all going to end, this crazy twisted mess they had made of their lives?

Presently she heard someone laughing and she wondered who it was. She sat up and then realized that she had been laughing. She laughed again. It was so funny that it deserved a lot of laughs. It wasn't every maid who got what her mistress wanted and then didn't have any use for it after it was given to her. Della had wanted a baby from the first. Ricky had insisted that they wait...

The phone rang but Della didn't bother answering it. Pretty soon she heard Jennie coming up the stairs.

"Mrs. Farland?"

"Yes?"

"Telephone."

"Thank you, Jennie."

Jennie came to the door and peeked inside.

"Sorry I frightened you," Della said. "I guess I—lost my head." The girl smiled.

"You've got reason to be mad, Mrs. Farland. I don't blame you one bit."

"Thank you, Jennie. And listen. I'm going to ask you to sign a paper. I'll tell you about it later."

She went to the telephone and lifted it.

"Yes?"

"Hi!" It was a man's voice. "Ed Loring: Hope I didn't disturb you."

"Not at all."

The phone wire hummed steadily.

"Anything new?"

Della smiled.

"Only that you were quite right. Hinting there might be changes around here."

"I'm sorry."

"Don't cry in your gin about it," she told him. "I'm not. In fact, I would have called you but I didn't have your number."

"You mean, about the camp?"

"Yes."

"You're interested?"

She could just see the look on Ricky's face when he learned that she was operating a nudist camp. Or the look on Gladys Anderson's face. Or Sally's. Or any of the other blue noses around North Landing and Port Jervis who liked to do what they shouldn't do when they were sure that nobody knew about it.

"We're practically in business," she told him.

Ed Loring whistled.

"Great! And when can I see you?"

She glanced down at the shorts and halter, wondering if this business deal with Ed Loring might not turn out to be as much fun as work.

"Anytime," she said. "Whenever you can make it."

"Well, get out your paper and pencil. Because I'm on my horse!"

She laughed, told him goodbye and hung up.

On her way out of the room she noticed Ricky's picture on the dresser. She crossed over and turned the picture about so that it faced the mirror.

4

EARLY MONDAY MORNING Tom Fielding called her and on Tuesday afternoon Ed drove out and took her into town.

"Everything's going to be settled today, huh?" Ed wanted to know.

"Well, not everything. Just the property, that's all."

Ed glanced at her and winked.

"That's enough to put us in business."

Della nodded, watching the green hills slide past the car. They had been over the proposition half a dozen times, figuring out the best place on the property for the reservation itself, matching the money she had and their initial expenses again and again.

The car slowed and Ed touched her elbow with the tips of his fingers.

"Believe me," he said. "It can't miss. It would be different if we were starting a new camp, because it would take time to get a following, but this group is already established. As soon as we can get the tents and set up the cots we'll be pulling in money."

She asked him something then that she had never asked him before.

"Ed—are you a nudist?"

"When I have to be."

"What do you mean by that?"

"I mean, I don't practice nudism like the believers do. I just take my clothes off whenever I go on the reservation. There are two reasons for that. First, most nudists feel that if you want to come where they are, you should act like them. And, secondly, I found that when you wear clothes among a lot of naked people that you feel self-conscious."

"Sounds funny."

"Maybe. But it isn't. Wearing clothes on a nudist reservation is like going without them on the street. All concerned feel mighty uncomfortable."

They came down the long hill, approaching the Landing. The Delaware River stretched to the south, winding through the valleys like a watery snake.

"As I've told you before," Ed said, "I'm honestly sorry about you and Ricky."

"It couldn't be helped."

"That was the secret I didn't want to share with you the other night. But I knew you soon might be interested in making a little money. Sally told me what was going to happen. That girl's a little tiger, Della. She may look small and soft but she's as hard as a keg of melted nails."

"I wish her luck."

"Oh, they'll do okay," Ed assured her, "They'll make a go of it."

Della had told Ed that she had five thousand dollars in the bank and that she was getting the property from Ricky. They both knew the five thousand dollars wouldn't last forever, even though she had cut down expenses by letting the gardener go and just keeping Jennie.

"How many people did you say were in this Camp? What is it?'

"Norcut." He lit two cigarettes and handed one to her. "Norcut Health Camp. Only we won't call it that up here. We'll call it—say, Raven's Nest Health Resort. If that's all right with you, of course."

"I don't care."

"As long as the money comes in?"

She laughed, feeling gay.

"As long as the money comes in."

His hand touched her arm, lingering, his fingers making a web of heat on her flesh.

"Let's go over the profit end of it again. I get fifty percent," Della said.

"Yes."

"And I give you twenty percent of that as your share."

"Right again."

"And the people who operate the reservation itself the Holdens—they get the other' fifty percent and they give you twenty out of that."

"Correct."

"That suits me," Della said. "And at my own house, if I want to keep people overnight I keep all the receipts?"

"Absolutely. That's your privilege."

They entered North Landing and Ed slowed the car for a stop light.

"Oh, you're going to like it!" he assured her, his fingers tightening. "You'll meet some great people. You know, some of the finest folks in the country are nudists. And the Holdens—well, both Arch and his wife, Betty, are pretty swell."

"You mentioned a daughter."

"Ada? Well, Ada is all right but sort of—nuts, if you ask me. There's also a brother, Mike, but he doesn't come around very often, so you won't be seeing much of him."

Della could have moved away from Ed's hand but she just looked down at it, smiling.

"You'll be able to call them as soon as I get through at the lawyer's," she said. "The place will be mine then, all mine. After all, I didn't want to order those tents and start spending money and then have Ricky back down on his word."

"Of course not."

"But Mr. Fielding said Ricky signed all the papers even before he told me."

"Sounds like he was anxious."

"Or very sure of himself."

Traffic was getting heavier as they moved downtown, and Ed needed both hands for driving purposes. But when he stopped, waiting for a car to back out of a parking spot, he looked at her, and his dark eyes probed intimately,

"Ricky must be blind," he said. "Or crazy. Or a little bit of both."

Ed was looking directly into her face but she was pretty sure that he was really watching the quick rise and fall of her breasts under the yellow sweater. The sweater was much too tight, and for this reason, she was, at the moment, wearing a brassiere. Not because she needed it for support or because it made her comfortable but because Jennie had told her that the sweater stretched apart and showed too much.

"You'd be better off stark naked," Jennie had said.

Della was pleased that Jennie was now reconciled to the idea of having the baby. She acted like a different girl these days, joking at meals and singing as she went about her work in the house. Her Sammy, she said, was in complete accord with her new plans.

"Where's that office again?" Ed asked.

"In the Palmer Building. That's the third block down, on this side."

North Landing was a small town, by no means as large as nearby Port Jervis, but it was prosperous enough during the spring, summer and fall months. In the spring people came to fish in the lakes and streams, particularly for bass and trout, and in the summer people just drove up to get out of the city. During the fall there was plenty of hunting and drinking at the camps scattered throughout the hills. Of course, in the winter it just died. The people who made money off the tourists spent the cold months in Florida and the ones who worked for them and helped them make the money crawled around in the snowbanks and somehow suffered out the cold.

"That must be it down there," Ed said, nodding at the red brick building with the clock hanging over the sidewalk.

There was a space near the corner and Ed pulled the Pontiac into that.

"Don't bother with the meter," Della told him, getting out. "That MD sign on the back plate is better in this town than a nickel."

Ed grinned and stretched.

"Sally'd flip her lid if she knew what I was doing with her old man's car."

Della went down the street, smiling. Ed was all right, she thought. Maybe he didn't have any money and maybe he'd never make very much, but he was nice to be with. What was it Ed had said? Oh, yes, Ed had told her that nudists felt that clothes gave people inferiority and superiority complexes that shouldn't exist. It was, she decided, pretty much the same with money. Money gave people inferiority and superiority complexes that were unfair and unreasonable. When a person got right down to it, down to the basic reasons for living, a man and a woman didn't need a great deal of money. All they had to have were healthy bodies and a sane and sensible outlook. No, she thought, money wasn't life. In fact, life might be very interesting with a man like Ed.

Della climbed the stairs to the lawyer's office, scolding herself mentally. She'd have to stop thinking about Ed Loring in that sort of way. Of course, Ed was a nice guy and she liked him but that was as far as it ought to go. Once Ricky, too, had been gentle and kind and at times fumbling, it had been almost wonderful. But later, when he had begun drinking and she knew that there had been other women—he had only disgusted her. She had felt like a shoddy piece of merchandise that no one wanted, just an extra thrill in Ricky's life when she should have been the most important.

She came from a country where people lived and loved. It wasn't something that could be shut off as easily or as quickly as a dripping faucet. Maybe, even, it was something that couldn't be shut off at all, she thought, as she paused at the lawyer's door.

There was one thing she had to make up her mind to right now. Perhaps she was different from other girls and perhaps that had been the cause of her trouble with Ricky. It was also possible that she was not frigid but, rather, too warm—no, not that, exactly, but possessed of some hidden desire that demanded more of a man than he was willing to give. Whatever the trouble was, whatever her difficulties, she must remember that this was a business arrangement with Ed Loring and nothing more. Ed Loring, she promised herself, would not be the first after Ricky.

Going into the office she felt better. She had made a decision about how she was going to handle Ed. She knew what she was going to do and how she was going to do it.

"May I help you?"

The girl who arose from behind the desk was tall and very thin. Her glance traveled up and down Della's voluptuous figure, lingering at the bustline. Della noted the look of envy and she wondered, not really caring, if the poor thing had a man of her own.

"I'm Mrs. Farland."

"Oh, yes, Won't you go right in?"

Della passed through an open doorway and found herself in a rather dark office lined with hundreds of books.

"Mrs. Farland?"

Tom Fielding was short and fat and hopelessly bald. He filled the chair behind the desk to overflowing and every time he moved the chair squeaked.

"Yes."

"Won't you be seated, please?"

Fielding had a low, pleasant voice and a friendly smile. Della sat down and he regarded her with mildly curious blue eyes.

"Sorry to hear about you and Ricky, Mrs. Farland. These things are always unfortunate."

"Yes."

"Naturally, when he first approached me just last week I had quite a talk with him. A lawyer's job, you know, is to serve the wishes of his client but it is also to help guide him, too. Often we make mistakes, mistakes, we wouldn't make if we had the advice of an outside party."

"I understand."

"But Ricky seemed very definitely unhappy. He—I might say, Mrs. Farland, that he is being very generous in view of the fact that he seems to blame you for any misunderstanding. I don't know, but sometimes—"

"I'm in a hurry," Della interrupted. "If you don't mind, I'd like to get this over with."

"Oh, yes. Yes, of course." Fielding leaned forward, pushing a stack of papers and a pen toward her. "Just sign where I have made the little check marks. Four places only. It's your title to the property and the furniture within the house at Raven's Nest."

She scanned the documents carefully. They seemed to be in order and she signed them quickly.

"Two copies for you," the lawyer said, sorting out the papers. "And two copies for me."

"All legal?"

"All legal." As she rose to go, Fielding waved his hand. "Just one more thing, Mrs. Farland, About the divorce. Your husband has retained me to handle that. It could be—well, rushed a bit if you would be willing to take a trip to—let's say, Reno."

"I'm not taking any trips."

"Oh ... I see." The fat face looked disappointed. "Of course, if you don't want to, you can't be forced into it. Only thing is it would speed matters a bit. Mr. Farland seemed very anxious to get the situation cleared up as quickly as possible. I think that makes a great deal of sense, if two people are going to part. They might as well get it over and done with."

"I'm not going anywhere," Della repeated firmly.

Fielding shrugged and got to his feet.

"Very well." Once more he waved at her. "One more thing. Quite frankly, I assume this to be an amicable divorce no court fights or that sort of thing. On the other hand one never knows and, therefore, I would like to have you sign this statement before you leave, certifying that you will not contest the divorce."

Della turned at the door and smiled at the lawyer.

"I'm not signing anything," she said sweetly.

Tom Fielding seemed to lose his poise.

"But Mr. Farland called me Sunday and said that you had agreed. When I drew up the papers on the property, it was with the understanding your husband was very emphatic about this—that the transfer was to take place only if you consented to the divorce. Then, on Sunday, he phoned me—from out of town, I think and he said that I could go ahead."

"Well, tell him you didn't do your job right," Della suggested. "Tell him you should have had me sign that other paper first."

Frustrated, Fielding lumbered across the room toward her.

"But, surely, a gentlemen's agreement—"

"Perhaps you have forgotten," she told him, letting him get a good look at the yellow sweater, "but I am a woman. A gentlemen's agreement means nothing to me. Besides, I promised nothing. He just assumed I did—in his usual headstrong fashion. Good afternoon, Mr. Fielding. And thank you for having been so careless."

She was still laughing when she reached the car. Ed Loring leaned across the seat, opening the door for her, his eyes questioning.

"Got it?"

"Got it!"

He started the car. "Now, let me at a telephone! Just let me at one of those things!"

His excitement was contagious, and she felt it mounting within her.

"Now we can get the tents, Ed. And you know that big one we talked about? The one where they cook and eat. We can put it by the lake."

The tires squealed as they went around a sharp corner. They broke out of traffic and swept out of town. His right arm circled her shoulders, pulling her close to him.

"I'll call in the order from the Nest. The stuff will be here in a few days."

"So soon?"

"And I'll get in touch with the Holdens tonight, after dinner. They're never around until then. As soon as the tents arrive they can start moving in." His arm grew tighter and she could feel his hand stroking her. "We'll be making money by the end of the week, Della! You hear that?"

It occurred to her that she would only have twenty-four hundred dollars left in the bank after paying for all of the things they needed. "I can hardly wait," she said truthfully.

The muffler on the Pontiac snarled as they climbed the mountain. Della remembered her decision of a few minutes before and she moved away from Ed's arm. This was strictly a business proposition. That would have to be enough for both of them.

When they reached the house Jennie met them at the door. She had on a red bathing suit and Della noted that the girl's condition hadn't yet begun to show.

"I thought I might go down to the lake," the girl said. "If it's all right with you."

"You go ahead," Della said. "Relax. The sun will do you good."

"Thank you, Mrs. Farland."

It was cooler in the house and a lot more comfortable than outside. Ed asked if it were air conditioned and she said, no, it was just insulated all the way through.

They went on into the living room. It was a large room, very light, and the huge picture windows overlooked Lake Sorrow. There was a fireplace at one end, with a hand hewed oaken mantel, but that was the only rural aspect of the whole place. The furniture was strictly modern, some of it real bamboo, and the rug was thick and soft and red.

"Fourteen tents," Ed said, sitting down by the phone. "Isn't that what we figured?"

"Not including the big one."

"No. But that comes from another place. And cots. How many of those?"

She tried to remember. Was it six times fourteen or eight times fourteen? And then they had added some for the house, in case there was an overflow.

"I don't know," she said. "It's upstairs. I've got it written down some-where. I'll get it."

"Okay. But hurry. If we put the order in right away they can start getting it out this afternoon."

She ran up the stairs, her heels clattering. What the hell had she done with that paper? She must have left it on the dresser or maybe it was still in the pocket of the jeans she had been wearing. But she couldn't find it anywhere. Anxiously, she kneeled and dug through the waste basket. The windows were open and a hot breeze drifted through the room. The more frantic her search the hotter she felt. What in God's name had she done with it? And why didn't either she or Jennie remember to close the windows in the morning? It was so much cooler with the windows closed. She swore bitterly and kicked the waste basket aside. Ed would be furious; she should have put that thing where she could find it.

She sat down on the bed and tried to remember what she had done with that stupid paper. She tried to remember what it looked like. A Kleenex? Hell, no, who'd be silly enough to write on a Kleenex? A napkin? Well, maybe a napkin. They'd been in the kitchen and they'd had a couple of cans of beer and it could have been a napkin. But somehow—no, now she remembered. Ricky had left the monthly bills piled neatly on the kitchen table and they'd done their figuring on the back of the envelope from the telephone company.

"Damn!"

Della got up from the bed and started for the door. God, she thought, but it was hot! And that sweater—anybody who wore a prickly thing like that in the summer ought to suffer.

She pulled the sweater up over her head and threw it on the floor. Deciding that the skirt was quite unnecessary now that she was home, she slipped out of that, too. As she moved toward the dresser, thinking that the pink shorts and pink halter would be best, she unfastened her brassiere and sighed contentedly as her breasts pushed out naked and free. The thin net panties swung with the rhythmic roll of her hips and her body felt wildly alive and glowing.

"God!" somebody breathed.

She wheeled quickly, feeling shame and panic, knowing that it was Ed.

She folded her arms across her breasts, trying to cover them. "You had no right to follow me!"

He stood in the doorway, his face almost white.

"You were gone so long," he said lamely, wetting his lips. His eyes moved away from her, then back again, lingering. "And I wanted to get that call in. That's all. Honest. I thought—"

"Well, you don't have to stand there, you know."

His eyes wandered down over her body, drinking in all the softness, caressing her flat little belly, the outward flow of her hips.

"You're very beautiful," he whispered, not moving.

Della smiled at him, now feeling neither shame nor fright. He was like a little boy who had followed the teacher into the cloakroom and who ought to be scolded. And, like the teacher, she was not alarmed. She would treat the incident lightly, making fun of him, and then it would never happen again.

"You told me that nudists believe all bodies are beautiful," she reminded Ed. "You told me that it didn't make any difference if they were young or old bodies, that each was the temple in which the soul lived and for that reason was always beautiful."

Ed wet his lips again, nervously. He took a cigarette from his shirt pocket, fumbled with it and then put it away again. °

"Sure," he admitted without much feeling. "Sure, I said that."

She continued to smile at him, to make him feel small, to make him want to leave her alone. He had followed her up the stairs and into her room, perhaps by accident or perhaps by design. It made little difference why he had come. He was there. And she had to make him leave, feeling guilty, just the way the teacher would make her pupil leave the cloak room.

"I guess you just don't make a very good nudist, Ed."

His stare lifted to her face, slowly.

"What makes you say that?"

She moved her arms, keeping her breasts covered.

"Because you can't look at nude women the way you're looking at me. You have to be the way you said, Ed you have to be disinterested. Aloof, I think you told me."

He continued to stand in the doorway, and she could see the sweat running down his face.

"I meant all of that," he insisted.

"Then remember it," she told him, still smiling. "Remember it not only while you're in the Camp but while you're here in my bedroom, like this. You remember that, Ed, and we'll get along fine because there won't be any chance of getting something else mixed in where only business belongs."

Ed stepped into the room. His shirt was soaking wet and his face was now fiery red.

"Well," he said huskily, "I hadn't seen you, when I said those things." He came toward her slowly. "And you've changed them, Della. Whether you like it or not you've changed all of the rules for this guy."

"Ed!"

The heat from his approaching body reached out and washed over her. The back of her head began to pound and hard pain crept into the breasts and her legs hurt.

"Please, Della!"

She closed her eyes, trying to think, pleading with her mind to rip destiny from the wants and the needs of her body.

"We'd better not," she whispered.

Suddenly, she wanted to laugh, to cry, to scream. And she wanted to run. She wanted to run because, in that moment of panic, she knew that she hungered for Ed Loring just as much as he craved her.

His arms circled her, crushing her flesh into his chest, his lips seeking and finding her mouth and forcing it open. They stumbled to the bed and fell upon it, clinging together.

"You knew this would happen," he told her.

She felt his hands, savage and urgent, demanding every response that the fire inside her body could possibly bring forth. The world and the moment closed in on her, spinning, whirling, driving her up to a pinnacle of pain and beauty and then down into a tunnel of blackness in which she heard only his frantic pleas and her own happy sobs of fulfillment.

Later, as she lay there upon the bed beside him, she knew that she had been right all along. Ed Loring was quite a man.

5

THE HOLDENS ARRIVED late Friday afternoon, dragging a huge red trailer behind their Buick station wagon.

"A very nice place you have here," Holden observed, nodding in the direction of the lake.

"I hope you'll like it," Della told him.

Arch Holden was in his early fifties, so short that he appeared squat. He had thin gray hair and an extremely high forehead. His wife, Betty was small and slim and her ageless face and long black hair gave her an illusion of youth.

"You're Mrs. Farland, aren't you?" She had a soft, pleasing voice.

"Yes. But please call me Della."

"Well, thanks. And I'm Betty." She winked at her husband. "Arch isn't very good at introducing me around. He likes to joke about it and say that he can't seem to recognize me with my clothes on."

Arch Holden laughed and gave his wife a tender kiss on the cheek. Then, glancing around: "Where's Ed?"

"He's down on the reservation. They're getting the rest of the tents set up this afternoon."

"And where's the reservation?"

Della walked with them to the front of the car, pointing to the lane that twisted down through the field, skirted the lake for a short distance, and then plunged into the woods.

"Any fields beyond those trees, Mrs. Farland?"

"Yes. Two."

"That's fine," Arch Holden said. "One of the prime requirements for a nudist reservation is plenty of good outdoor sport. Of course, we won't be able to get very much started for a few days but we do have badminton and croquet stuff in the trailer. The grass would have to be mowed down quite good, though."

"It's already been cut," Della stated proudly.

"Where can we swim?" Betty Holden wanted to know.

"The lake is private," Della told her. "It belongs to me and no one else lives near it. We have another pond, too, a small one down there in the woods, but there are a lot of snapping turtles in it and we've never used it."

"We'll stick to the lake," Arch Holden said.

The Holdens got into their car, saying that they would see her later, and the big trailer began moving slowly forward. Della watched until it entered the woods, bobbing and weaving, and then she returned to the house.

Jennie was in the kitchen, scraping cheese off the electric sandwich maker.

"That's the way to travel," Jennie said flatly. "In a trailer. If you don't like what you see, you don't stop, you just keep on going."

"Maybe you're right."

I'm surprised that Mr. Loring hasn't got one, that's for sure. He's a pickup-and-goer if I ever saw one. I know the kind. I seen them down in Port, that one year I worked there. They're all nice, just like him, but it don't make any difference if they're selling magazines or working on the railroad, they're all the same. Pick up and go. That's what they do."

There were times, Della thought, when Jennie could be most annoying.

"By the way," Della said to the girl, "I have that paper made out for you. I'd like to have you sign it."

Jennie began to scrape harder on the sandwich maker.

"You mean, that one about Mr. Farland?"

"Yes."

"Well, I haven't asked Sammy about it yet, Mrs. Farland."

"Oh, you haven't?" Della demanded icily. "And why haven't you?"

The girl looked at Della, her eyes pathetic.

"I will tonight," she promised. "Honest."

"Look," Della said patiently. "Sammy isn't the one to blame for your condition. Mr. Farland is, Mr. Farland is the father of your child, Jennie, All I ask is that you sign a statement that says he is responsible."

She'd written the paper out in longhand and she'd gone over it twice with Jennie already. She was getting a little sick of it.

"I know," Jennie admitted. "Only it's just that I always talk things over with Sammy first, that's all. That way—"

"There's one thing you didn't ask Sammy first, Jennie. You never asked him if it was all right for Mr. Farland to do what he did, did you?"

"Now, Mrs. Farland—"

"You 'listen to me!" Della went over and stood very close to the girl. "Supposing you do have this baby and supposing something should happen to you. It could, you know. You could die!"

"Oh, no!"

"Well, it's happened before. Haven't you ever thought of that? You could die and then, Jennie, who'd take care of your baby? Haven't you ever thought of that?"

Jennie pushed the sandwich maker aside and leaned up against the sink. Her face was alarmed, her body limp.

"No, I never thought of that," she said. "You told me before that you'd make sure the baby—"

"And I will, Jennie. I'll see that your baby will be cared for no matter what happens. But I want what you know on paper and I want it signed by you. Then if anything happened to you, or to me, Mr. Farland would have to take care of it, wouldn't he? And, Jennie—tell me, Jennie, wouldn't that be the fair and right thing for Mr. Farland to do?"

Jennie hesitated.

"But it might cause trouble, Mrs. Farland."

"It won't."

"I mean—"

"The trouble's already been caused," Della reminded her.

"I guess."

Della reached into the pocket of her shorts, finding the neatly folded paper and the pen. She shoved the pen into Jennie's trembling hand and put the paper on the countertop.

"You read it before, Jennie."

"Yes, Mrs. Farland."

"It's the truth?"

"It's the truth."

"Then, sign it."

"But, Mrs. Farland—"

"Sign it!"

A couple of tears dropped to the white sheet as Jennie slowly and carefully signed her name. Jennie Slater. Jennie Slater, Della thought, age almost twenty. Jennie Slater, an unfortunate little kid whose signature might yet prove as potent as that of a bank president.

"You won't be sorry, Jennie," Della said.

"I hope not."

Della returned the paper and pen to her pocket.

"There's something else I wanted to talk to you about, Jennie."

"Yes, Mrs. Farland."

Della went over to the kitchen table and sat down. She felt hot and tired. She guessed that she and Ed had been staying up too late nights together. She smiled. Maybe it was love and maybe it wasn't but it was real and beautiful, no matter what it was, and even if she did feel tired.

"You know how to drive a car, Jennie?"

"Yes."

"And you've got a license?"

"Yes."

"Good. We've got to get a car, Jennie. Nothing fancy, just something that will take us into town and back. Or Port Jervis. A few of our guests may come up on the train and we'll have to meet them."

"I like to drive a car," Jennie said. "Sammy lets me drive his sometimes."

"We can get Ed to take us in this afternoon and pick one out," Della said. "Ed says that Sally Berringer's father wants his station wagon back and I can't say that I blame him. We've been using it now most all week and he's been pretty decent about it."

"Oh, that puts me in mind," Jennie exclaimed. "That Miss Berringer called on the telephone a little while ago."

"She wanted Ed?"

"No, You."

"I'll call her later," Della said. "If I don't forget."

"She didn't say what she wanted."

"No." Della lit a cigarette and watched the smoke drift toward the door. "Now, about that car, Jennie. I can't afford a new one but I would like to get one that you'd want to drive. I'm no good at driving, myself. I used to drive, back home—those little English Consuls and a real old

Plymouth—but we drove on the left hand side and I'd kill myself if I ever got out on a road around here."

"You don't have to worry none," Jennie promised. "I'll do all the driving you want."

"I plan on paying you a little more money," Della said. "Starting next week. You're going to have a lot more work to do, Jennie. We're opening a nudist camp," Della told her.

Jennie's eyes were startled.

"Nudists," she repeated. "That's people without clothes?"

"Yes."

"Men or women?"

"Both."

"Holy cow!" Jennie exclaimed. "Wait till Sammy hears about this!"

"You can tell him. It isn't any secret."

Jennie glanced out of the window and snickered.

"He'll flip his lid," Jennie decided. "It'll be the last thing in the world that he ever expected to hear."

"A lot of other people will probably feel the same way about it."

"A nudist camp," Jennie repeated. "You're not kidding me, are you?"

"Of course not."

"Well, I'm not taking my clothes off and running around stark naked," Jennie announced firmly. "That's for sure, Mrs. Farland."

"You don't have to worry about that, Jennie. You'll just work here in the house, the way you do now, and drive the car. Of course, we'll have people staying up here, off and on, and it'll be your job to see that the rooms are clean and that they get something to eat."

For a moment she thought that Jennie was going to shrink into a corner and disappear through the woodwork,

"Not naked, Mrs. Farland! They ain't going to be up here in this house, running all around without—"

"No, Jennie. Everybody will be dressed up here. The only place where people can go nude is on the reservation, down past the woods."

Jennie appeared to be somewhat relieved.

"Well, I'm never going down there," she vowed. "I don't want to be seeing no naked men. And I don't want no men seeing me."

"All right, Jennie. Just don't let it upset you."

"Oh, it's okay," the girl said hastily. "Long as I can stay up here and them down there." She returned to the sink, glancing back at Della, "You ain't going down there without no clothes on, are you, Mrs. Farland?"

"I suppose I may have to sometimes."

The sandwich maker fell out of Jennie's hand, clattering in the sink. "Honest?"

"You can't be dressed when you go on the reservation," Della explained. "They claim it makes the nudists self-conscious."

"Well, I declare!" Jennie breathed. Then she smiled. "I sure hope that Mr. Loring never catches you with your clothes off, Mrs. Farland. He ever finds you that way and there's a good chance of there being two of us like me."

"Jennie!"

"Sorry, Mrs. Farland, but I was just saying." Chimes suddenly sounded.

"Somebody's at the front door," Jennie said, drying her hands on a towel.

"I'll get it," Della said, rising from the table.

A couple was standing on the front porch. Both were in their early twenties, and very tanned. The girl had rich brown hair and soft gray eyes. Her companion was about the same medium height with wide, powerful shoulders.

"I was looking for Mr. and Mrs. Holden," the man said.

"They're down on the reservation."

"Oh, fine!"

"Just follow the road around the house and then take the lane past the lake."

"Good enough."

The man turned to go but the girl lingered.

"You must be Mrs. Farland?"

"Yes, that's right."

"I'm Audrey Potter." She pulled at the man's shirt sleeve. "Butch, meet Mrs. Farland. Mrs. Farland, Butch."

"Hi," he said. Then, in the direction of the car, a red and black convertible with the top up which was parked in the roadway: "Ada—say, Ada, come on up and meet Mrs. Farland."

The girl who got out of the car and came toward them was tall and slim. She had jet black hair, long and wavy over her shoulders, and her face was a creamy tan. Her legs, beneath the tightfitting black dress, were long and bare and brown. She walked with a lazy, unrestrained motion that made her pelvis roll from side to side. As she came up the steps onto the porch the dress dipped low in front and Della could see the twin high mounds of her breasts.

"This is Ada Holden," Audrey Potter said. "Ada, Mrs. Farland."

"Greetings," Ada said. The bright red lips parted in a smile. "I guess the folks got here all right."

"They pulled the trailer down to the reservation."

"Fine. And did they go over the details on the arrivals with you?"

"No, but Mr. Loring did."

"I see." The red lips parted again, revealing small white teeth. "Then you know that you should have everybody register when they come in? And I suppose you have a book for that purpose?"

"Yes, I picked up one in town."

"I suggest that you register only couples," Ada said. "Or families, if any come. We have to be careful about that, you know, because if we accept any unmarried men or women the purpose of the Camp might be misinterpreted."

"Mr. Loring explained that to me."

"Oh. Well, I thought he had, but I wanted to be sure, that's all."

At first, Della hadn't been in complete agreement with Ed's instructions. He'd said that engaged couples should be treated as married couples, that a "couple" simply meant a man and a woman. He'd pointed out that most of the people who came to them would be sincere, honestly interested in the nudist movement, and it would be easy enough to pick out the lone man or woman who should not be admitted. To question their guests too severely, he had pointed out, would prove offensive. The main thing was to be on the alert for undesirables and to safeguard the name of the Camp at all times. Recognizing the logic of his views, Della accepted them.

"One other thing," Ada Holden was saying. "It might be a good idea if you put a gate out here by the house. That way no one can get in without you knowing and no one can get out without paying."

"I'll talk to Mr. Loring about it."

"I can hardly wait to get out of my clothes." Ada's smile flashed again. She lifted one hand and unfastened the two buttons at the top of her dress. The material fell away, exposing the dark wedge between her breasts and the pink brassiere. "I hope everything will be ready, Mrs. Farland. We should have a good crowd this weekend."

"They've just about finished putting up the tents."

"We'll have at least a hundred people."

Della's mind began running up totals like an adding machine. A hundred people meant a hundred dollars a day ground charge. Fifty percent of that was fifty dollars, less ten for Ed, which would leave her forty. This didn't, of course, include the daily charge for meals—four dollars per person of which she was to receive half and pay half of the food bills—or the three dollar-a-night bunk charge of which she was also to receive fifty percent.

"Aw, come on, Ada," Butch pleaded. "Let's get down there and get unpacked."

"You can register us if you will," Ada said, descending the steps. "Just Audrey Potter and Butch Culver. You don't have to bother about me, not unless you want to. But don't expect any pay. We're all part of the overhead."

They got into the car and drove off, waving back at Della.

"Mrs. Farland!" Jennie was hollering from inside the house. "Miss Berringer is calling you again."

Della sighed and went into the living room.

"I'll take it in here," she said picking up the phone. Then: "Hello, Sally. How are you?"

"You're a bitch," Sally whispered brokenly.

"Calling me names won't do you any good."

"Bitch!" Sally repeated. "I saw Mr. Fielding last night and he told me you wouldn't give Ricky his divorce."

Della looked up at the ceiling, letting her wait.

"I simply said I wouldn't consent to it," she told Sally finally. "He can have it if he wants to fight for it. That's up to him."

"You just wait until Ricky gets back! You just wait, you, you—"

"I'll wait," Della said and hung up.

She picked up the registration book and opened it, but Jennie yelled again.

"There's another car out back, Mrs. Farland. Some fellow who acts like he don't know where he's going."

"Ask him what he wants."

She heard Jennie shouting to somebody, followed by a brief silence.

"He wants a room," Jennie said.

"We don't take single people," Della advised her. "Tell him we're sorry."

"Okay."

Ricky, she thought, remembering the telephone call from Sally, how do you feel now, you and that sly little doctor's daughter? Della slammed the book shut savagely. She hated him. Who the hell did he think he was? And, when you got right down to it, what good did it do for a girl to live right, to try to make a home? People laughed at her. That's what people did. They laughed at her and poked fun at her and called her an iceberg. An iceberg, was she? Ed Loring didn't seem to think so. Maybe Ed could tell Ricky what his wife was like, what she was really like. That miserable Ricky and his little Sally snip, who did they think they were?

"Am I intruding?"

A man stood in the doorway, smiling at her.

"No. Of course not. Come on in."

He was a nondescript little man carrying several leather cases.

"I realize that you don't rent out to single folks," he said, putting the bags on the floor. "Just as the girl out there told me. However, I have a note from Mr. Holden which I am sure you'll find satisfactory."

The man handed her a slip of paper and she glanced at it. It requested that the man be given a room and it was signed by Arch Holden.

"All right," Della agreed. "Rooms are seven dollars a night."

The man seemed surprised.

"That's a little high."

Della ignored the protest and opened the large book.

"If you would register, please."

"Oh. Oh, yes."

He came over and wrote in the book. It was impossible to read his name, almost as though he had deliberately obscured it.

"Pay in advance?"

"If you please."

"Not taking any chances, are you?" He smiled and handed her a ten and a five, "I'll be here two nights."

"There is also a grounds charge of a dollar a day."

He put another bill into her hand, a one.

"There is one thing I should like to ask," he said. "I want to be absolutely certain that no strangers can go into my room. I wouldn't want anything to happen to my gear."

"You mean those bags?"

Della's guest looked offended.

"Those bags," he explained, "happen to contain some very expensive photographic equipment. At least fifteen hundred dollars' worth."

"Well, nothing will happen to it," Della assured him. "You can keep it in your room and lock the door when you go out."

"Thank you very much."

"Jennie!" Della called in the direction of the kitchen. "Jennie, would you be kind enough to show this gentleman to his room. You know the one I mean, Mr. Farland's old room."

The lodger went upstairs with Jennie and Della passed through the kitchen and on outside.

Ed was just walking up the lane. His clothes were covered with caked mud and water stains and dust.

"Well, we got 'em up," he announced, grinning. "Every last tent pole."

"You must be bushed."

"I'm on fire."

"How about a beer?"

"Sounds good to me."

They walked together toward the house,

"And what about the mess tent?" Della wanted to know. "Did you get that up too?"

"Sure. Even got the stoves hooked up. Only we didn't put it anywhere near the lake. Somehow, it didn't seem quite private enough. So we stuck it in that field, the one past where we put up the sleeping tents."

"I'd like to see the place." Della said. "Must be like an army camp."

"We'll go down tomorrow," Ed told her. "Together."

She felt her face color.

"It'll seem funny," she decided. "Real strange, going into a nudist camp."

"Aw, you'll get used to it in no time at all."

Inside, Ed got beer out of the refrigerator and opened two cans.

"Arch and his wife were very pleased," Ed reported. "They said this is one of the nicest spots they've ever seen. And Ada, too. She thought it was the greatest."

"That's good." The bitter taste of the beer filled her mouth. "You know something, Ed? We ought to get into town this afternoon and get a car."

Ed nodded.

"And guess what?" she asked, remembering the money the man had paid her. "I rented one of the rooms already."

"I thought I recognized Ken's car out there."

"I think he's a photographer."

"That's right."

"But he won't take any pictures, will he? I mean, I wouldn't think anybody would want—"

"He'll just snap those who want their pictures taken," Ed said, finishing his beer. "And that'll be most of them, Della. People are odd that way. And since we don't allow any cameras to be brought into Camp by the guests, Arch has Ken on the staff to accommodate those who are interested."

"I see."

Ed crossed the kitchen and put the empty beer can on the sink.

"You know, that's a good idea about the car because I've got to take the doc's back this afternoon. We could leave Jennie here to check in the arrivals while we run down to the Landing."

"I'd rather Jennie went with you," Della said. "She'll be driving the car most of the time and maybe it would be better if she picked it out. I'll stay here and check them in."

Ed came over and kissed her full on the mouth.

"You're a good sport," he said.

Her eyes found his and held.

"I want to be."

"We won't be long. We'll get hold of something."

"I'll give you a check. But don't spend more than five hundred."

"Hell, we ought to get something pretty good for that."

Jennie came in and Della sent her up to change. Ed washed up in the sink and Della tried to brush off his clothes with a paper towel.

"I'll bring my clothes and stuff back from town," he said. "Maybe I can use one of the rooms upstairs."

"You know you can."

He kissed her hard and for a moment she clung to him. Jennie and Ed left for the Landing shortly after that, and they had hardly gotten out of sight before the cars began to arrive in earnest.

They were a strange assortment of men and women, old and young, short and tall, fat and thin. A few had children with them—laughing, shouting kids who tore through the house while their parents registered. In less than two hours, more than eighty people had disappeared down the lane, their cars bumping through the dust.

Della wondered, vaguely, what they would all look like with their clothes off.

By this time tomorrow she would know.

6

THE MORNING WAS hot and sticky, the red sun rolling up into the sky like a giant ball of flame. A white sail stood motionless at the far end of Lake Sorrow and overhead a pair of hawks circled lazily.

"Everybody is taken by this setting," Ed said. "It couldn't be more beautiful."

They were walking down the lane, toward the woods. Ed had wanted to start out earlier but Della had been obliged to help Jennie with some of the work—all the bedrooms had been occupied the night before and one arrival had even slept on the couch.

"Close to a hundred people here already," Ed said. "And we'll have more by tonight. Tomorrow, though, some will check out and then during the week it will fall off to about fifty or sixty."

"But we'll still be making money," Della said.

Ed grinned at her.

"That's what I like about you. You've got a cash register for a mind."

She felt his hand on her arm, a warm and hard and a capable hand. She needed that hand.

Last night she had admitted it to herself, lying there in bed. She hadn't been able to sleep and she had wanted Ed so badly that her legs had ached. Once she had heard him coming along the hall and had thought he was going to knock. But he had passed her door without touching it. It had been a long night, a lonely night, and she had kept asking herself if she was different after all. Maybe she wasn't like other girls—normal girls who didn't think of a man in that way. Or did a normal girl, if there was such a thing, have the same thoughts and simply not divulge them to anybody else? What was so wrong, anyway, with wanting a man? If a person needed a drink of water, they took it. If they were hungry, they ate. And if they needed love—well, if they really had to have someone to love them, why shouldn't they satisfy that appetite, too? Oh, of course, she was still Ricky's wife but it was just a word, a silly title. It didn't mean anything, not anymore. And it never had, really. Ricky with his foul mouth, his beatings, his drinking and his other women. How could that be love? How could any woman be satisfied with that kind of love? And how could a woman keep herself happy without some kind of love?

"Ed," she said. "I'm nervous. I don't know whether I can do this."

"Della?"

"What, Ed?"

His hand slid away from her arm, moving around her waist. They walked along very close, very slow.

They were near the lake and she could smell the water, fresh and clean. A bass broke the surface, chasing a bug, and thousands of tiny fish leaped in alarm.

"There's nothing to worry about," he said. "Every thing's going to be fine. But I'll admit that it's hard the first time. It always is, Della."

"Don't leave me." She was surprised to find herself, somehow, rather afraid, every nerve in her body tingling. "Stay with me."

His hand squeezed her.

"You don't have to tell me twice."

She could now see the cook tent through the dark shadows of the trees, its tan top reflecting the bright sun. A deer fly buzzed close to her hair and as she jerked her head away Ed kissed her on the cheek.

"Where do we—undress?"

"I knew that was bothering you," he laughed.

"Not in the open, I hope."

"No, he said. "You have some privacy even in a nudist camp. You undress by yourself, dress by yourself and go to the john by yourself. In all else, though, it is one great big group movement."

"But where?"

He smiled.

"You mean, undress?"

"Of course, silly!"

"Well, there's a tent. for men visitors and a tent for the women. The more or less permanent people have their own tents."

The heat in the woods was damp and oppressive and the pine needles crunched under their feet. As they neared the clearing she could see tents, and wash hanging out on several lines. She could smell coffee, beef roasting in a pan over a charcoal fire. And she saw several people there in the clearing walking around as naked as the day they had been born.

"They play games in the morning," Ed explained, kicking a marsh-mallow box out of the way. "In the afternoon they usually lie in the sun or go swimming. But you have to be careful on a day like this, unless your skin is heavily tanned already. The sun can burn you and if you get too much of it at first it can make you very ill. People who have been nudists for years never have that trouble. They get so brown that the tan hangs over from one year to the next. I know nudists who look, during January, as though they just got back from Florida and, hell, the farthest south they had been was the Staten Island ferry."

They had reached the clearing. He led her toward a pair of tents immediately to the right.

"Yours is the first one, that's for ladies. And I'll use the other. Just leave your shoes on, that's all. Some people don't, but this isn't very good walking around here barefooted. And you'll find some hats inside. Bring one with you. You'll need it to keep the sun out of your eyes and, besides, it's the only place you'll have to carry your cigarettes and matches."

She stopped in front of the tent, her heart beating rapidly.

"I'll wait inside for you, Ed."

"Okay."

He walked off and she entered the tent. It was very hot in there and the only light was the rays of the sun which seeped through the canvas. She noticed two ropes strung down either side, holding clothes that were kept fastened with spring-type clothes pins.

"Hello, girl."

The woman who sat on a camp stool in one corner was old and fat and ugly. The extent of her wearing apparel was a pair of faded blue sneakers. Her breasts hung down like gourds on an aged vine and the heavy flesh across her stomach folded down over her upper thighs like a sack. Della remembered seeing the woman when she'd registered and had thought then that the visitor looked rather trim for her age. How much could a girdle lie?

"You're the lady from the house, aren't you?"

"Yes," Della said.

"We were wondering if you'd come down."

"Well, I got this far," Della admitted. "But the rest of the way looks pretty rugged."

"Oh, shucks!" The woman stood up, the flesh of her body sagging all over. "Lookit me, girl. Lookit a damned, ugly horse if you ever saw one. And does it bother me? Not in the least. I go out there and hell around with them just the same."

"You must be used to it," Della acknowledged, unfastening her halter.

"You never get used to it, girl. There's them who says you do and there's others—like me—who say you don't. You just never do, that's all. I don't care what that Holden says in his lectures, or what anybody else says, there's something about some of the human bodies you see—that gets you."

Della placed the halter upon the line and stretched, her breasts plunging forward and out and alive.

The woman laughed and plodded over to her.

"There's them that'll really be interested in your body, girl."

She flushed and unfastened her shorts. They were tight across her buttocks and she had to tug on them. She could feel the woman's eyes watching her every movement as she pulled the shorts down over her legs and stepped out of them.

"You're very beautiful, girl. And, like I say, you'll have plenty of them standing on end. You go to one of Holden's lectures—he's gonna have one in a couple of minutes—and half the people there won't be listening to him. Some of the women will be looking at you and trying to find something wrong with you, trying to figure something they have that you haven't got. And the men—well, you know how men are. They can prattle all they want to about a naked man looking at a naked woman and not having an idea in the world, but it just isn't so. The only time that people don't have ideas is after they are dead, girlie."

Della pinned her clothes on the line and then went to the front of the tent, waiting for Ed.

"You make it sound—dirty," she told the woman. "And it isn't that way at all."

"Oh, no?"

"No!" Della flared angrily, her full breasts heaving. "Of course it isn't. This isn't exactly new to me, you know. In my own country, in Iceland, boys and girls and men and women often went swimming together— without any clothes. And we used to take sunbaths together, to get the good out of the sun. Nothing wrong happened there and nothing wrong is going to happen here!"

The fat woman sighed and slowly lit a cigarette.

"No hard feelings," the woman said. "I was just testing you, that's all. You've got the right spirit. And you'll have a good camp."

A shadow moved across the front of the tent and stopped.

"Hey, Della! You ready?"

"Close your eyes." She laughed nervously. "You close yours and I'll close mine."

"All right."

And she did close her eyes as she pulled back the tent flap and stepped outside, entering a new world, a world of starkly naked flesh. A world where people lived and breathed and talked and did as they pleased. A world that was a throwback to the age of primeval man. A world of sunlight and respect and clean fun. The world of the nudist. A world that would be part of her future from this moment on.

"Della!" Ed's voice was husky. "You are beautiful!"

She kept her eyes closed, smiling up at him, the sun burning down, remembering, and not caring, that she had forgotten to bring the hat.

"Am I, Ed? Am I beautiful?"

For answer he kissed her once on the cheek, lightly. She felt his hands touch her shoulders and move away, touch and move away again.

"You can open your eyes now, Della."

"In a second."

There was a short silence.

"I'm not wearing any clothes either, Della."

She smiled again and the sun blazed across her skin. She wasn't afraid now, not sorry, not anything. The warm air flowed around her body—not hot, just warm and filled with life—reaching every tiny secret cell. The rays of the sun drove into her skin, burying themselves in her flesh, pumping into her blood a feeling of luxury and freedom that she had not known since leaving Iceland.

She smiled again and opened her eyes.

Ed was beautiful, too.

Her eyes regarded him in frank speculation. Then she took his arm and they walked away from the tent.

They went over to the badminton court where two men and two women were playing up a storm. A rather large group of onlookers shouted instructions and good natured insults.

"Everybody has fun," Ed told her.

It was strange, she thought, but she had looked at Ed just that one time, there by the tent, and now she stood unselfconsciously with Ed beside her, strong and brown, and that was all that seemed to matter. It was all out in the open.

A few minutes later, while Ed was over talking to some short guest with a lot of hair on his chest, she remembered what the fat woman had told her. The women, she decided, were looking at her with some display of jealousy, especially the older ones. Or was it admiration? She didn't know. And the men—well, to be frank with herself, she would have been unhappy if the men hadn't looked at her. After all, she did have a young and beautiful body, didn't she? And what woman didn't yearn to be admired by the male of the species?

"Mrs. Farland?"

She turned and found herself facing a boy of about twelve.

"I'm Sidney Barnes, Mrs. Farland." The boy's eyes were soft blue and very bright. "My daddy—he's playing badminton over there said to tell you what a nice place you have. He said for mommy to do that, too, if she saw you."

A sense of accomplishment swelled within Della's bosom.

"Thank you," she said. "Thank you very much, Sidney."

She watched the boy run off just as a shout went up from the crowd and the badminton match ended.

Ed returned and stood beside her.

"It's a good crowd," he said. "And they're enjoying themselves."

"Yes."

"And they all like you, which is a help."

"I think I like them," she said, seriously.

A whistle blew sharply and Della jumped.

"Lecture time," Ed laughed. "There's a lecture given every morning on the benefits of nudism. Of course, the old hands have heard it all before but they like to hear it again. I guess it's a little bit like listening to your favorite political candidate."

The men, women and children began moving across the field toward one of the towering maples.

"You ought to hear one of these talks," Ed told her. "Arch and his daughter can put on a spiel when they're in the mood."

They followed the crowd.

"I really ought to be getting back to the house," Della said.

"Getting cold feet?"

"No. Surprisingly, I feel just the other way about it."

He smiled and got cigarettes out from under his hat. He lit two and handed one to her.

"I keep forgetting," he said. "This isn't new to you. You probably saw more nude bodies in Iceland than most of these people will ever see."

"Well, it isn't quite the same," Della told him, thoughtfully. "I don't know just how to say it, but—in Iceland, Ed, it is quite a natural thing while. here, in the States, it seems to be a challenge, something to do that others are afraid to do."

They stopped under the shade of the big maple. Arch Holden, not looking at all like he had in clothes but more like a small brown bear, stood in the middle of the large semicircle. To his left was his daughter, Ada, and when Della saw the girl she let out a little gasp of astonishment. Ada, without any exaggeration, had the most perfectly formed body Della had ever seen. Her legs were long and delicately shaped, her hips wide and soft, her stomach was very narrow with just the hint of a bulge at the naval and her breasts were full, wide apart and jutting. Long black hair hung down almost to her shoulders, blowing gently in the breeze, and her red lips were parted in a wet, provocative smile.

"She's lovely!" Della breathed. ~

"You must mean Ada."

"Yes."

"Well, I'll give her credit for that," Ed agreed. "She's got the shape of a Hollywood star."

Della glanced at Ed sharply. She couldn't decide whether his voice had been edged with hate, distrust—or love. And his face, now smiling down at her, told her nothing.

Arch Holden began to speak. He said he wished to welcome everyone to the new camp, and to thank Della for her hospitality. Then commented on the many new faces present.

"New faces are as welcome as the sun to a nudist," he said. "New faces mean that more and more people are seeking the benefits of nudism. They mean that more and more people recognize the merit of our movement, want to assemble with us to enjoy the great outdoors."

"He's a corker when he gets going," Ed whispered. "Like a seven-day-clock with a ten-year mainspring."

"The value of the sun," Holden went on, "has long been recognized by the medical profession. Take the ray treatments used in hospital therapy, for example. Ultraviolet and infrared rays are used to help rebuild tired bodies, to bring new life to old cells, to make sick people well again. These rays are found in sunlight. Why, then, does the medical profession—and the law—often frown upon the practices of nudism?"

A hush had settled over the crowd.

"The law says," Holden continued, "that it is not right for the human male to view the human female in the undressed state. Why, then, is it right for a male doctor to treat female patients? Why is it right for a female doctor to treat male patients? In both cases, the patient often must undress. You ask the law, folks. Don't ask me. I've figured and figured and I'm damned if I know why it is."

"Make sense to you?" Ed wanted to know.

"Yes."

"Now, take the sun," Holden 'was saying. "There are seven colors in the rays of the sun—seven colors whose wavelengths the bodies of men and women need. And in clothes we don't get them. We get barely enough to keep alive and that's all. If you don't believe me, put a person in a totally dark room and keep him there. See how long he lives. It won't be long. He'll soon die. And, why? I'll tell you why. Because he didn't get any sun, that's why. You ask any doctor and he'll tell you it's so. He'll admit it. And then he'll tell you that a camp such as we have here is wrong, that it's immoral. You tell me who is nuts. You tell me, folks!"

"The damned law," one man said. "It oughta be changed."

"Of course it should be changed," Holden agreed. "But I'm not going to keep you here all morning talking about it, All I do in these lectures:

is tell you a little bit more about nudism, each time, and ask you to think about it. I'm asking you to do that today. And I'm ask ing you to think about one thing in particular. Do you believe that in groups such as ours—everybody the same, no mysteries—that there could possibly be as many sex crimes as in similiarly sized groups fully clothed? Of course not! And I said sex crimes; I did not say sex acts. The sexual act is the very foundation of the human race and anyone who disputes it is disputing their right to live. If anyone believes that sex is degrading, that it is something that should be hidden, then they them selves should go into hiding. Because they themselves are the result of the union of a man and a woman."

Holden terminated his lecture with the same suddenness with which he had begun it. For a few moments the people kept standing around, as though waiting for more, and then they started to drift away.

"Arch should have been a politician," Ed said. "He'd have had Congress sitting around in bare skins."

Della burst out laughing. "Just the thing, in a democracy."

They walked back across the field and when they got to the dressing tents Ed gave her a little kiss on the back of the neck.

"You get your clothes on and run along up," he said.

"I've got some things to take care of and I'll join you later."

"For lunch?"

"Maybe."

He kissed her again and then she pushed the flap back and stepped inside the tent. She dressed with distaste. The clothes gave her the feeling of being bandaged from head to foot.

A few minutes later she left the tent, hurried through the woods and met Jennie coming down the road near the lake.

"I wasn't going all the way down there," Jennie said hastily. "Not me, Mrs. Farland, But I just had to find you."

"Why? What's wrong?"

"It's Mr. Farland," Jennie exclaimed breathlessly. "He come charging into the house and he wanted to know where you were. I—I've never seen him so mad." Jennie clasped her hands firmly together and her eyes were frightened. "That's why I just had to find you, Mrs. Farland.

To tell you to stay away from the house. The way he is well, it's hard to say what he'll do."

"Where is he now?"

"In the kitchen, when I left."

"All right," Della said, her voice steady. "I'll talk to Mr. Farland, if that's what he wants."

Jennie tried to hold her but she pushed the girl's hand away.

"He's awful mad! Honest he is! If I were you, I wouldn't—"

"I'm not afraid of him," Della said. "I'm not afraid of him one little bit."

She walked quickly up the road toward the house.

7

RICKY WASN'T IN the kitchen, but she heard him moving around in the living room.

"Ricky!"

He turned and faced her as she came into the room. He flung a magazine out of his hand and strode toward her.

"I see your reading habits have settled into the sewer, he said.

The magazine had fallen face up. She saw it was a nudist monthly which the man who had occupied the couch had been reading.

She hadn't looked at the pictures or thought about the magazine. It hadn't meant anything to her one way or the other.

"That isn't what you came here for," Della said. "To criticize my reading."

"You're a damned poor sport," he told her, "I called Tom Fielding the other night and he told me what you'd said, how you'd acted. I—I couldn't believe it." Ricky's tone was angry, his eyes very dark. "I hadn't taken a drink, not all week. And I hadn't had much luck with the fish. But I kept telling myself that I'd already drunk enough for two lives, that I had to cut it out, that I had to pull myself together."

"Not for me," Della reminded him bitterly. "For Sally."

"Well. Sally, sure. And for me. For my own sake." He turned away, shaking his head. "But you don't care. Hell, you don't give a damn. When Tom told me—I couldn't believe it! Oh, I was sore at Tom, of course I was. I'm still sore. But it isn't all his fault. You behaved dishonestly, baby. You backed down on an agreement."

Ricky was different, she thought, now that he was sober. There was none of his drunken arrogance, none of the sureness usually characterizing him. He looked fit, though, his eyes and skin both clear.

She heard someone coming down the stairs and she crossed the room. It was the photographer, dressed in swim trunks and sandals,

"Hi, member," he said to Ricky. Then, squinting at Della, "You better be sure about that stuff being all right. I lose that equipment and I might as well drop dead two minutes after."

"I told you it would be safe, didn't I? Stop worrying. Enjoy yourself."

"How can I do that?" he wanted to know, pushing open the screen door. "Half the fun in life is worrying."

"Who's that character?" Ricky demanded.

"A roomer."

"You must have a lot of roomers, baby. There's about nine million cars out back."

"Well, I've got a lot of—uh—roomers."

He came toward her, feet shuffling on the thick carpet.

"Della, what are you hiding? What's going on? You'd better tell me, or—"

She faced him squarely. She had determined how she was going to do this, how she had to handle him. For the first time since she had known Ricky she struck him. She slapped him full across the face with her right hand. His head snapped back and she could feel the sting go all the way to her elbow.

"You have no right to ask questions of me any more," she told him savagely. Her face was deadly white. "This isn't your home, Ricky. It's mine. You gave up all your rights in it the day you walked out on me. So don't ask me who's here and who isn't—or anything else. It's none of your business."

The red marks of her fingers marred one side of his face. He sneered at her.

"You little bitch!" he stormed. "You damned hussy!"

She hit him again, on the other side.

"And don't call me names. Don't ever call me names again, Ricky Farland. You've been cursing at me for a year and I'm sick and tired of it. You've called me every stinking, rotten name you could think of—but I'm not going to listen to it any more. What do you think you've been talking to, anyway, a piece of furniture? You think I have no feelings, that those things don't hurt me?"

Surprise filled his eyes and he backed away from her, fumbling for a cigarette, his shoulders slumping.

"Now, baby, look here—"

She tossed the hair out of her eyes and stepped closer to him.

"And don't call me baby, ever again! You hear that, Ricky? Never again! You call me that name once more and you'll wake up thinking you married a wildcat."

He rubbed his face thoughtfully, staring at her.

"Maybe I did," he said.

It started coming out then, all of it, all of the pent-up hatred fostered by his abuse. She hadn't ever wanted to say it, to put it into words, but he was there and she hated him and she couldn't help herself.

"So now I'm a wildcat. Is that it? Before, I was an iceberg, or a fish head, or a fish tail, or a whore, or some other terrible thing. The only difference was in how much you had to drink, whether you'd had fun with some other woman—you hear me, Ricky—or how you wanted to humiliate me in front of other people."

"For God's sake, Della!" Ricky's face was ashen. "Knock it off."

She could feel it inside of her, swelling up, churning in her blood like flood waters in a river. She wanted to get it finished and over and done with, to cut the rope that had tied them to cut it so clean, so certainly, that no one, nobody, would ever be able to splice it for them again.

"Knock it off!" Della threw back her head, laughing. "Knock it off. Is that all you can ever think of? Knock it off? What about Sally?" she demanded, brutally. "Did you ever knock that off?"

"Della, I'm telling you—"

"You're telling me nothing," she raged. "I'm telling you. I'll give you the house,' you said. 'I'll give you the money you've got in the bank,' you said. Just a great big generous—"

"You got all that, Della. You know you did!"

"Shut up. I know why you were so bighearted. I know… nobody told me, but I know. I don't have you to thank for it, but Sally. I know what she said, just what I would have said. "You can't just kick her out, she said. "What would people think?' Yes, what would people think, and gossip about? Ricky Farland, the big shot, kicking out a girl he dragged more than three thousand miles to marry. No, you couldn't just kick me out, Ricky, because some of the people you know—some of those who are important to you socially—might not buy that kind of treatment. Some people still believe in some sort of justice and you're just smart enough to know it. So by giving me something, by being so bighearted, you make yourself out a hero and you turn your wife into a bum."

Ricky wheeled and flung the cigarette into the fireplace.

"I never saw you like this before. Hell, I thought we could sit down and talk things over. I thought—"

"There's nothing to talk over," Della assured him. "You signed you'd give me the house and the money and I'd use up the money and I wouldn't know what to do. You know the Icelandic consul here can't help anybody, except to put him on one of those terrible fishing boats and send him back home. You know that, Ricky. You know it and that's what you wanted to happen to me. But it won't, you hear me? It won't happen at all. Even if you hadn't given a dime—even if you had kicked me out—it still wouldn't have happened. Because I'll work, Ricky. I'll work and I'll earn money and I'll never be the helpless fool you think I am."

"Look," he said, spreading his hands wide. "Look, why can't we talk this thing over?"

"I tell you, there's nothing to talk over. You said it all before, Ricky."

"Listen to me, will you?" He wandered over to the couch and sat down. "You don't understand, Della. I've got to have this divorce. I've got to!"

"Well, then, go ahead and get it!"

"You could make it easy for me," he insisted. "You could go somewhere and get it quickly."

"No, thank you!"

"Della, please!" His tone was desperate. "You don't understand. It's money." He hesitated, looking straight at her. "I'm broke, Della. Broke!"

"Broke?" She was genuinely shocked. "I don't understand. You—"

"The taxes took a lot," Ricky explained wearily. "And the business wasn't worth anything at all. I thought it was. But with half of the equipment in Iceland and the other half on the way, the outfit wasn't worth a strong breath. Not when the work there canceled out and we didn't have any other jobs to do. Just an office, not even worth the time it took to unlock the door and close it again."

"But you must have known," Della protested. "All this time."

"You still don't understand, do you? You don't understand what it's like to have a lot of money and then find out you have nothing at all.

It was hard for me to believe money wasn't there any more. Oh, a little cash was around for a while. But now every cent is gone."

"You wasted enough of it."

He stood up, his face coloring.

"Sure. This house and the cars, your bank account, your maid—"

"I wanted at least that much out of this marriage," she flared. "I wasn't getting anything else."

"And you were right about the women," he said, ignoring her. "There were a lot of them. But it was your fault, Della, just as much as it was mine."

"Don't blame me!"

"But I do, partly. It was one of those things you read about yet don't believe. You can't see how two people, a man and a woman—well, you get things about that in the mail sometimes. The psychologists call it a lack of adjustment, or some other such silly thing, but maybe that's as good a word as any other. I read once that just a change of climate could do it, create tension. I hadn't thought about it until this last week, not at all. And then when the fish didn't bite I got to thinking. I wondered if maybe—but, what the hell? What's the use of talking about all that now?"

"None whatever," Della replied.

"Then just give me that divorce," he said. "It isn't fair of you to stand in my way."

"What is fair, then?"

"That you give it to me. That you don't act like this."

"And let you go just like that?" Della demanded.

"It doesn't matter. We don't mean anything to each other, any more."

"I don't argue that."

"So there's no sense to what you're doing. Not a bit."

She turned her back on him, deliberately.

"You want me to make it easy for you to marry Sally, is that it?"

"That's part of it."

"And the other part?" Della probed. She looked out of the window, down across the lake. No sail was in sight but she could see Jennie down there along the shore, skipping rocks on the water. "It's money, isn't it? You need money. And you can't get any of it until you get the Berringer name behind you. And you can't use the Berringer name until you've used Sally. Or have you already used her?"

She could hear only the sounds of Ricky's heavy breathing. He did not answer.

"That's the deal, isn't it, Ricky? I should have guessed before. I should have realized she was buying you. But if you need money so badly, why don't you go to your sister? Gladys has plenty. Won't she help you?"

He had stepped closer to her. She could hear his breathing.

"Won't she?"

"Gladys would," Ricky said finally. "But that husband of hers, he's a slob. To hear him talk, you'd think that being a doctor is the only important thing in life—even if you're unsuccessful at it. He keeps saying he doesn't want to live on his wife's money, but do you know what? He's living on it all the time. Why, he doesn't make enough even to pay for the fancy equipment he's bought. Not half enough. You think he'd let her lend me any dough? You think he'd take a chance on losing some of it? You're as nuts as they come if you think that."

Ricky, she thought, Ricky, you fool, you've really gone and loused things up. You've made a mess of things from start to finish. Only you're not finished yet. As a matter of fact, you haven't even started yet, Ricky!

"Della, baby." His hands suddenly were on her shoulders, pulling her body close. "Now, don't get sore," he said quickly. "Don't get angry at me. I don't call you 'baby' to irritate you. It's just that, well, it's sort of natural, it's what I just naturally like to call you—"

"I don't like it."

"I know that." His fingers gripped her shoulders. "I know that. But you've got to help me, Della. You can't let me down now. I was born in this town, brought up here. This is my home. Maybe it isn't your home but it's my home. I have to make a living here. And I have to have a chance to do that. All I'm asking you for is the divorce. I'm not asking you for one other thing. Hell, if you need some money I'll even start giving you some as soon as I'm making it. I can't right now, but maybe later on I can. Whatever you want I'll give you. So help me God I will, Della. But I have to have that divorce. Do you understand that? I've got to have it!"

"I understand," she said. She raised her hands, loosened his fingers, and moved away. She picked up a cigarette and lit it slowly. "Only you're not getting it, Ricky. And another thing—" She smiled. She would give it to him now. She would give it to him good. She would give him so much that he would never want to come back for more. She'd drive it into him, like a spike, and every time he looked inside himself, he'd see the wound. He'd see the wound and he'd know that she had put it there and that it would never, never heal. "That man you saw coming down the stairs," she continued. "He's a nudist."

"A what?"

"A nudist. You know, a person who runs around without clothes on."

"The hell you say," Ricky breathed.

"And those cars out there, the ones parked.in back. All those cars belong to—er—nudists."

Ricky looked stunned, as though she had struck him with a claw hammer.

"The field past the woods is filled with them, darling. If you don't believe me, go and see for yourself. You might even find a woman down there that would appeal to you. There's one who's a real goddess."

"Holy cow!" Ricky said finally, staring at her. "Do you know what you're doing?"

"Of course I know."

"Nudist!"

"That's right."

"It's—why, it's against the law!"

"Oh, no it isn't. Not in New Jersey. Not so long as they behave themselves and mind their own business."

"I don't believe you."

She shrugged. "You know I never lie."

He took out a cigarette but he didn't light it. "What will people say?"

"Who cares what they say? I don't."

"But I do!"

"I'm sorry," she said, not sorry at all. "That's too bad."

He dropped the cold cigarette to the rug and kicked it aside.

"So that's it," he said. "You're going to make as much muck as you can and you're going to drag me through it."

"I hadn't thought of it that way, exactly—"

"The hell you hadn't!" His eyes challenged her. "You've got it all figured out, haven't you? You started this nudist camp or outdoor brothel or whatever it is"

"Ricky!"

"—and you know it'll kick up a stink. And you know that as long as I'm married to you, whether I want to be or not, that a lot of people are going to think it's just as much my fault as yours. But it isn't going to work that way, baby, it isn't going to work that way at all."

"It isn't?"

His eyes tore at her, desperate.

"You're damned right it isn't!" His voice rose to a shout. "I'll drag you into court—I'll drag you into a hundred courts, if I have to—and I'll get that divorce. You see if I don't. If it's a fight you want, it's a fight you're going to get. Because you're not going to stand in my way. I'll walk over you like you're so much dirt under my feet! A nudist camp! Why, you miserable slut, it's just the ticket for you."

She waited a long while, just looking at him, her breasts heaving, before she spoke again.

"So it's a fight you're going to give me?" she wondered.

"You know it!"

"And what do you think your Sally will say to that?"

"She wants my divorce as much as I do."

"Even if you have to fight me?"

His smile was crooked.

"Even to a fight."

"And what will she say about all the—filthy things that will come out?"

"Everybody will know about your nudist camp by then, anyway. And the other things won't make any difference."

"I see."

He moved toward her. "It's up to you," he said. "Entirely."

She looked up into his face and laughed. She would give it to him now, all the way. She'd opened up the wound and now she'd salt it.

"You said Sally wants the divorce as much as you do."

"That's right."

"Why?"

"Why! If you're already married you have to get a divorce before you can get married again, don't you? Only an idiot would ask a question like that."

"Oh," Della said, demurely, "I thought she might be in the same condition as Jennie!"

"She might—what!"

"You heard me."

"You must be nuts," Ricky said. "Absolutely nuts."

"Yes," she repeated, "Like Jennie. And you made her that way, Ricky. Only you're not going to get away with it. Not for any lousy two hundred dollars. Not for a lot of dollars. You're never going to get away with it. I have a paper that Jennie signed, and it says that you're the father. You're going to pay, Ricky Farland. You're going to pay and pay and pay. You're going—"

"You crazy bitch!" He was waving clenched fists.

She backed away from him hastily.

"Take it to court," she dared him. "Take the divorce to court and I'll wreck you. I'll drag out every bit of dirt that you fouled yourself with."

"Bitch!" he said between his teeth.

"I'll teach you," she promised, still backing away. "You'll learn—the hard way."

His face was livid. She could see a giant pulse beating just beneath his chin and he rubbed his hands across his eyes. Huge beads of sweat dripped from his face and disappeared into the carpet. He was moving toward her.

"You bitch," he kept repeating. "You miserable bitch!"

And then, quite suddenly, Della felt a wave of terror sweep through her, twisting every jagged nerve. Some thing inside of Ricky had torn loose. His mind was running wild. She could see it in his deadly, unblinking eyes, the knotted curl of his fingers.

"Get out of here!" she screamed frantically.

"You bitch," he said again.

He wasn't shouting now. He kept saying the word over and over, as if he were memorizing it. He began to straighten, his shoulders squaring. A nerve twitched at one corner of his mouth.

"Ricky! For the love of God!"

She wanted to run but she couldn't. Desperately she looked away from him. Where was everybody? Where was Jennie? And Ed. If Ed were only with her. But he wasn't. Nobody was. And she was scared.

"Ricky! Please. God, Ricky!"

He hit her with his fist, full on the mouth, driving her backward. She stumbled, not feeling any pain at all, and went sprawling to the couch.

"Bitch!" he shouted, following her.

"No!" She became aware of the salt taste of the blood and her whole face began to ache, "No, Ricky!"

He grabbed her hair, lifting her. She thought he was going to strike her again and she closed her eyes, afraid of what she would see if she didn't. His face, she didn't want to look at his face. She couldn't! It was the face of a man gone mad, of a man struggling down a fearful and lonely road. Or, perhaps, that of a man at the end of such a road.

"I'll teach you," Ricky promised bitterly.

He grabbed the halter, ripping it loose. She could feel the thin line across her back, like the sting of a whip, where the material had buried itself before breaking.

"You want to be a nudist," he grated as her naked breasts plunged into view. "I'll make you a damned nudist."

"I'll kill you for this!" she whispered furiously.

"Stand over there," he directed, "and let's see what the other fellows are looking at these days."

You'll pay for this, she thought. You'll pay big for this, Ricky.

"Get out of here," she told him.

Her eyes were open now and she could feel the swelling around the left one. Her mouth was sore and her nose ached,

"Not before I'm finished, baby." Again, he began stalking her. "I haven't even started yet."

The cold stone of the fireplace pressed into her back and she moved sideways, quickly, as he lunged. Her left hand sought and found the heavy iron logfork and as she whirled upon him she raised the fork high over her head.

"I'll knock your brains out!" she threatened.

His glance raced to the waiting fork.

"Hey, now," he said, retreating. "Put that thing down."

"I'll put it through your skull!"

The fork made a hissing sound as it swept through the air and downward. Ricky let out a shout and bolted for the door.

"Keep moving," she advised as he lingered by the door. "And don't come back. So help me God, I'll kill you if you do, Ricky!"

He stared at her uncertainly for a moment.

"I'll buy that," he said finally. "I think maybe you would,"

He opened the door.

"You're wrong about one thing," he said, looking back at her. "Jennie. I didn't have anything to do with Jennie. She told me she needed money and I gave it to her. That's all there was to it."

"And you're a liar!"

The hinges of the screen door squealed.

"You've sure got a pair," he remarked and spat on the floor.

The door slammed behind him and his footsteps went over and down off the porch. Slowly, her body shaking uncontrollably, she rested the fork against the side of the fireplace.

She picked up the halter and looked at it. Torn beyond repair. In disgust, she threw it on the floor.

She turned, holding her head very high and fighting back the tears, and walked to the stairs.

By the time she reached her room she was sobbing.

8

THE STATE POLICE arrived early the following morning, Sunday. Ed had just gone down to the reservation and Jennie was in the kitchen worrying about carving four chickens for dinner.

"Honest," the girl said, "with all this business going on, we should have a cook, we should."

Della had seen the police car pull around back and stop. She waited until the trooper got out and then she went over to the kitchen door.

"We'll get a cook," Della promised. "If we're still in business after this man leaves, that is."

Jennie joined her at the door.

"Lordy!" she gasped. "I'll bet we won't be. I'll bet somebody's going to get in a lot of trouble about all these naked people around."

The trooper came up on the porch.

"Mrs. Farland?"

"Yes. I'm Mrs. Farland."

"I'll go upstairs and make the beds," Jennie said hastily.

Della went out and leaned against the railing. The sun burned down hot against, the white shorts and white halter. Her face was still sore from Ricky's blow and it hurt when she smiled.

"May I help you?" she said.

The trooper stared at her from behind dark glasses.

"Well, I came up to investigate a complaint we've received," he said. "Frankly, I don't know if there's anything to it but we've been told that you're operating a nudist colony."

"Camp," Della corrected him. "We no longer call them colonies. They are camps. Health camps."

"Oh." The trooper seemed uncertain. "Then, you don't deny it?"

"Of course not." She moved away from the railing and went down the steps. "Naturally, if you wish to see the camp, you're welcome to do so at any time."

The trooper removed his dark glasses and grinned.

"You mean that?"

"Why, certainly."

"Well, I don't know about that," the trooper said. "I was just sent up here to find out about it."

"It's up to you," Della said. "We have nothing to hide."

"Well, I'm damned!" the trooper stated incredulously. "A nudist camp!"

"There's nothing wrong about having a nudist camp up here," Della explained carefully. "I mean, there's no law against having one. Just against indecent exposure, officer. And there is none of that here."

"Not that I've seen," the trooper agreed.

"The reservation is beyond those trees, past the lake, and it's all private property."

"I see."

"It wouldn't seem as though we're violating any law, would it?"

The trooper shifted his weight from one foot to the other,

"No, I guess not."

"We mind our own business and we expect other people to mind theirs."

He came down and stood beside her. His glance was curious,

"Are you—Mrs. Farland, are you a nudist?'

"I own the property," she explained. "And I do practice it when I go on the reservation, but that is all."

"You mean, you have to take your clothes off when you go down there?"

Della nodded.

"I'll be damned!" The trooper took a deep breath and his gun belt creaked.

"We want to abide by the law," Della assured him.

"Oh, I think you're doing that all right. As you say, the law concerns itself with indecent exposure and there doesn't appear to be any of that around here."

"Thank you, officer."

"It just sounds kind of crazy, that's all."

"What does?"

"People running around with their clothes off." He shrugged. "But everybody to their own way of doing things."

The trooper turned abruptly and started toward the black and white Ford.

"Officer?"

"Yes, Mrs. Farland?"

"May I ask you who put in the complaint about us?"

"Somebody said it was your husband."

"I thought so!"

Ricky, she thought, you're a poor loser.

"I imagine somebody will be out from the Board of Health to look at your camp," the trooper said, getting into the car. He closed the door and looked at her. "Would a fellow—say, this old doc, the one that goes around to the summer places and who now says he wants to see the camp—would he have to take his clothes off, too?"

"He'd feel out of place if he didn't."

The trooper nodded thoughtfully.

"Yeah," he decided. "Yeah, I suppose he would." Then, as he started the car, he laughed. "Man, I can see it now! That poor old Doc Jergens, a rack of bones if there ever was one, running around in his birthday suit and lugging his big black bag. Boy, that would be the day!"

The trooper, still laughing, backed the car around and drove off down the road.

The trooper would have a lot of fun out of that, Della thought returning to the house. Most likely he'll head straight back to his station so he could tell the boys about it. Maybe he'd tell them all about the nudist camp and the naked women and a lot of other things that he'd never seen. And the "boys" would tell somebody else and eventually, the word would be around the whole countryside. By that time the camp wouldn't be a nudist camp at all but a seraglio under the trees and the stories would get bigger and nastier. After a while, the people would hear so many yarns that they'd get to believing them, and then the same people who had started the stories would be angry at the cops because the cops didn't enforce the law. It would still be the same clean camp for those who wanted to enjoy it, but it would be nothing but a sex farm as far as the gossips were concerned.

"Oh, Mrs. Farland! Mrs. Farland!"

A couple with two children were coming up the lane and Della waited for them, thinking of Ricky and how he had had encouraged the very thing he feared.

You fool, Ricky, you stupid fool, she thought. Now the rumors would start, and the tongues would wag, and filth would seep through the town. But, in the end, it would be the worse for him because he'd be in the town, not knowing if it were true, and she'd be up there in the hills, knowing that it was nothing but lies, all lies.

"Mrs. Farland," the woman said, "I'm afraid we'll have to check out."

The boy and girl ran around the house, chasing a butterfly, and the husband stood to one side, his face very white.

"So soon?" Della was surprised. "I certainly hope that nothing happened to displease you."

"Now don't you worry about that," the woman said, glancing at her husband. "It's Mr. Niles and his terrible ulcer."

"Oh, I'm sorry!"

"Don't be," Mr. Niles said. "The thing raises hell all the time and I thought the sun might help it. But it didn't, so I think I'd better go down to Trenton and see the doctor."

"But we'll be back," Mrs. Niles promised. "You have a lovely place here, Mrs. Farland. So well run. A person feels—safe."

"Thank you."

"It's more than you can say for some nudist camps," Mrs. Niles explained.

Della was about to mention the bill when Mr. Niles handed her a pair of twenties and told her it was close enough and that she should keep the change. Then the mother went about rounding up her children and Della waited until they drove off, waving after them.

She entered the house, feeling pleased. Let Ricky kick up all the fuss he wished to, let the cops come every day, as long as these people enjoyed themselves and were happy. Take the Niles family, for instance. A man and a woman with two growing youngsters, and they had been pleased. Not only that, but it was obvious that the children had been satisfied and that was most important. Children, especially those of preteen age, were often dubious about nudism. This was partly due to the fact that they had reached the age of body curiosity, the age when speculation and doubt were often misunderstood for the truth.

Jennie, somewhat breathless, met Della in the hall.

"I don't want you to think I was snooping," Jennie stated hurriedly. "I wasn't. I was just changing his bed, like I always do, and I flopped the mattress over and—"

"Whose bed?"

"Why, I don't know. That Mr. What'shisname. The man with all those things that we put in Mr. Farland's room."

"You mean, the photographer?"

Jennie's face darkened and she laughed.

"If that's what he does, he sure as hell takes some dandies," she said. "And if he don't take any pictures he must be in the collecting business. I never saw so many naked women in all my life. And men. Men, too. You'd hardly believe it, Mrs. Farland!"

"That's his business," Della said. "Taking pictures. And it's none of yours."

Jennie looked sullen.

"I'm sorry, Mrs, Farland. I just thought you ought to know."

"Well, I did know."

Jennie turned and went back down the hall, Della following. She'd have to make certain that the girl hadn't disturbed any of the photographer's material or he'd be furious.

Della entered the room. Photography cases were scattered all around, a shirt was thrown over the back of a chair and a pair of pants lay in a heap on the floor. Evidently the occupant had rinsed out a pair of socks and these were draped over the Venetian blinds, drying in the breeze. But Della saw hardly any of these things, or the bottle on the dresser, or the cigarette butts on the floor. She couldn't lift her stare away from the black springs of the bed.

"There must be a hundred or more of them things," Jennie said, "Dirty pictures, Mrs. Farland."

Della bent forward and examined the pictures. Some were of individuals, men and women, while others were either of couples or small groups. She recognized a few as people she had seen on the reservation.

"The dirt is all in your mind," Della told the girl, dropping the mattress back into place. "There's nothing wrong with those pictures."

"But they're all naked, Mrs. Farland!"

"And so are you,' Della told her on the way out of the room. "Twice a day. When you dress and when you get undressed. So if it's wrong for them it's wrong for you. The only thing they did was have their pictures taken."

Smiling, Della descended the stairs. People were funny, she thought. Really funny. To believe that a photo of the human body was immoral was to believe that every fiber and every muscle was a secret vice. Of course, she realized that her background and training were considerably different from those of an American because, in Iceland, even the magazines had a lot of nakedness in them. Not the type found in the States, not retouched stuff, but real natural nakedness. And the movies—well, a good movie in Iceland was the kind of a movie that left extremely little to the imagination.

Della sauntered into her own bedroom, walked over to the window and stood looking out. What a beautiful place, she thought, as her eyes caressed the wide, green lawn, the silver saucer of the lake, the magnificent towering, trees. How wonderful it was to look down there and know that at last she was putting her energy into something worthwhile, something that was real and vital.

Gaily, she turned away from the window and lit a cigarette. It was such a glorious, satisfying thing to be aware that she would not only earn a nice income through helping the nudists in their movement but that she might also be able to contribute something to a better understanding of their cause. Of course, Arch Holden and the others were nudists, but they were nudists by cultivation and acquired conviction rather than by natural inclination. They had not been brought up as she had, to accept the human body as a part of everyday living and to feel no shame in its necessary functions. True, they claimed to feel that way and they said that they did, but it was a manufactured belief, not a belief that came from deep inside.

Hastily she left the room and descended the stairs. She wanted to see Ed right away and talk to him about this. She felt that he would be pleased, that he would recognize her outlook, as she did, as a solid foundation upon which they could build the biggest and finest nudist camp in the States. A camp without mysteries, she thought. A camp that could give everyone the best in everything they might seek.

Outside, the sun burned down hot and steady. The grass was very dry, crackling, and she could hear the grasshoppers leaping for safety as she moved quickly down the lane. Just as she reached the lake a wood chuck whistled and scurried for cover and from the safety of the deep woods a blue jay scolded her soundly.

"Hot," an unclothed man said as they met in the woods.

"Very."

"Great place you have here, Mrs. Farland."

"I'm glad you like it."

She approached the clearing. Several people stood around a boy playing the accordion, and slightly beyond, a handful of onlookers cheered another badminton match. Della looked about for Ed but she did not see him. Nor did she see any of the Holdens. She paused only briefly, still searching, and then entered the women's dressing tent.

"Oh, hi there!"

Della blinked, driving the brightness of the sun from her eyes.

"Oh, hello," she said.

It was Ada Holden.

"Lovely day."

"Yes," Della agreed. Then, "Have you seen Ed?"

"No, but he's around somewhere."

"Thanks."

Della untied her halter and slipped out of it.

"There's one thing I've meant to ask you, Mrs. Farland." Ada leaned forward and cupped her breasts into a sheer net bra. "What do you think of the nudist camp business so far?"

"I think it's fine."

"Honestly?"

"Why, of course." Della's glance sought out the figure of the girl on the opposite side of the tent. "I think it's wonderful that people can observe their beliefs. And I believe it is healthy. I really do."

"Well, hell," Ada exclaimed, as the thin blue dress slid down over her body, clinging to every curve, "it sure feels good to hide your belongings once in a while. Sometimes I get tired of running around with all of me showing."

Della put the halter and shorts on the clothesline and fastened the pin in place.

"Anything you need from town?" Ada wanted to know. "I'm driving in."

"No, thanks."

Jennie and Ed had brought up the groceries the night before. She recalled now how disgusted she had felt when she'd first seen the secondhand station wagon, a '49 Ford with part of the woodwork rotted away. But she'd felt better about it when told that they had only paid one ninety-five for it, that the tires were good, and that the motor had been recently overhauled.

"I don't know how you feel about it," Ada said, "but, for my money, there isn't anything more disgusting than a naked man."

"I really hadn't thought an awful lot about it."

Ada sighed and hooked her stockings into place.

"No one could ever say that about you, Mrs, Farland." Her smile flashed and lingered. "You have a truly beautiful body. I am sure you are admired by both men and women."

"And yours is beautiful, too."

"Do you really think so?"

"Yes."

She left Ada alone in the tent and hurried over to where the lad was playing the accordion.

"No, Mr. Loring isn't here," a woman with a sagging chest told her. "Try the Holdens' tent, why don't you? That's the second one down, on the left."

But Ed wasn't there, either. Mrs. Holden, who was sitting at an upended trunk, writing a letter on a portable typewriter, said it was too hot for anybody to be around very much, anyway.

"Take a look in the fourth one down," Arch Holden suggested, sitting down on an ancient army cot. Almost in the same motion he yawned and stretched out wearily. "Maybe he's there."

All of the tents were the same with the exception of the fourth one and the only thing different about this was the sign—"Supplies, No Charge Accounts"—stapled on the flap.

"Ed!" Della called. "Ed Loring!"

The flap moved beneath her hand, and Ed's face appeared. He grinned and winked at her.

"Well, surprise!" he said. His eyes slid down over her body. "I thought you'd be up at the house."

"Ed, I just had to see you."

His grin widened and he pushed the flap aside.

"Well, come in."

She slipped through the opening into the tent. There was a table in the middle, with boxes piled high all around and a canvas partition about three-quarters of the way to the rear. Above the table a huge mirror, facing downward, hung from the ridge pole.

"First," Della told him, "the police were here."

Ed looked startled.

"And what happened?"

"Nothing. I think everything was all right."

"Fine!"

"Ricky is the one who turned in the complaint. And I imagine there'll be others."

Ed's face came very close and his voice was soft. "Not getting chicken, are you?" Della laughed.

"No."

Ed kissed her full on the mouth, pulling her in tight. Their flesh touched, fused for a moment and then she slipped away from him.

"I wanted to talk to you, Ed," she said seriously. "About the camp and a couple of other things."

He leaned up against a pile of cartons, watching her.

"Shoot," he said.

"Well, to begin with, Jennie found a bunch of pictures in that photographer's room."

"She must have been snooping."

"Oh, she was. But the point is, Ed, I don't think we should have a photographer on the grounds. It seems to me that if we don't have one and if we take only married couples or parents with children—well, there can't ever be any trouble."

"There isn't any trouble now."

"No," she admitted. "There isn't. But—"

"Look," Ed said, coming over to her. "I know how you feel because I feel the same way. I wouldn't want my picture taken and I'm sure you wouldn't, but we have to remember that a lot of other people go for a thing like that. Ken is hired by Arch to render a service to those who want it. Isn't it better to have a regular photographer on the staff than it is to take a chance on some nut sneaking a camera into the grounds?"

Della thought about that for a moment.

"I suppose you're right."

"Good." He put his hand under her chin and tilted her head back. "And as for the couples—you've seen the crowd we have here, Della. They're all nice folks. All of them. Maybe some of them aren't married. I don't know. All I know is that they behave themselves and that they act like ladies and gentlemen. I don't know what more you can ask from human beings."

"Not much," Della agreed. "But we do have to be careful, Ed. Honestly. If we should have just one little thing happen—just one!—it could cause us all kinds of trouble. And it would ruin something for both of us, something that can be very fine."

He kissed her again, harder this time, and she didn't try to get away.

"Don't you worry," he told her. "Nothing's going to happen."

"I just want to be sure."

"I'll talk to Ken about those pictures, I'll ask him not to leave them around any more. He ought to know better than that, anyway."

"All right."

"You just leave it up to me." His lips moved against her mouth. "You just leave everything to Ed Loring. You just do that and you keep on belonging to me and well both be happy."

She pushed herself up on her toes, returning his kiss.

"Oh, Ed!"

She let out a little cry as his big hand caressed her.

"You're beautiful."

She felt the rich strength of his body as he pulled her in closer.

"You're pretty, too," she said.

"Hell, a man can't be pretty."

She kissed him again, clinging to him as her legs grew weak and filled with pain.

"Only to a woman," she whispered.

He said something then, something wonderful and terrible and frightening.

"Fight me!" he begged. "Fight me!"

But she couldn't fight him because she wanted him so very much. Her hungry body became a part of him, demanding all of his love, and the sweet ecstasy of boundless intimacy possessed her utterly.

Time and the day stood still.

9

THE FIRST FEW days of the following week were very quiet ones. About seventy-five had checked out late Sunday afternoon, including the photographer, Ken Shoals, and the exodus had left but fifty-odd people at the camp.

"Just like when I used to work at a boarding house," Jennie remarked. "Break your back until after Sunday dinner and then it takes you until Wednesday to unwind."

Ed had stayed on, of course, as had the Holdens. Della had given Ed the bedroom nearest her own. Her door was never locked against him, a fact of which he took frequent advantage.

"Ed," she said to him Thursday morning, when he stopped in for a prebreakfast kiss. "Ed, you know, I've been thinking about something."

He yawned and sat down sleepily on her bed.

"Yeah?"

"About us."

His arm moved and comfortably circled her shoulders.

"Go on," he said. "Tell me more."

She patted his hand and sat up, her long, slim legs dangling briefly over the edge. Then she reached for the négligée at the foot of the bed, shrugged into it and stood up.

"This isn't any good," she said, looking down at his tousled hair. "And we both know it."

His eyes were dark and serious,

"You mean—enjoying each other, loving each other?"

"I mean living like this. You sneaking from your room in here and then sneaking back out again. It can't be what either one of us wants. People just can't go on living this way forever, Ed. It doesn't make sense."

Ed sat up and reached for a cigarette.

"I don't know why not," he said.

"I'm still a married woman," she reminded him.

"I know that."

She walked to the dresser, looking at herself in the mirror. Her skin was radiant, her eyes alive. She had not looked so well in years. Ed had done it for her. Ed had given her this beauty.

She watched his face in the mirror. He frowned and said nothing. She turned, smiling at him fondly. "I don't know what the answer is, Ed. I wondered if you did."

"That's easy," he told her, rising from the rumpled bed. "We could get married."

"But I am married."

Ed found his shorts and stepped into them.

"You could get a divorce," he said.

"Ah... And you'd marry me?"

"I'd marry you."

They had never talked about marriage before, not seriously, but the idea of it had been with her, haunting her every moment of the night and the day since that first time she had surrendered to him, She had accepted Ed Loring on a temporary basis but she wanted something for tomorrow, too. There was a fear in her. A fear that he might just be using her, that he might soon grow tired of her.

"I'd marry you anytime," he told her now, coming close. "All you have to do is be free. All you have to do is get a divorce, set the date and I'll be there."

An overpowering sensation of relief swelled up within her.

"Oh, Ed!" she sobbed and pressed up against him. "Oh, Ed, darling!"

He kissed her full and hard on the lips.

"You should have known that, Della."

"But you never said so."

"I said so just now."

She clung to him, trembling.

"Ed! You don't know how much that means to me."

"You're a little fool, hon."

"A stupid fool."

"A lovely fool," he amended. "Kiss me."

She kissed him on the mouth, her lips parted and hungry.

"I have been a fool," she told him. "You don't know how big a one."

And they as they dressed, she in the bathroom and Ed in the bedroom, she told him about Ricky and how he had wanted a divorce and how she had fought with him about it. She even told him about Jennie and the statement and how she'd held that as a club over Ricky's head.

"You're a hellcat," Ed told her earnestly. "You get a guy right where you want him and then you drive needles into him."

She came out of the bathroom, wearing a light blue dress that fit her perfectly, feeling gloriously alive and vital.

"I fight for what's mine," she said.

"I wasn't criticizing," Ed told her, kissing her on the neck. "You've got plenty of guts and I admire that."

"But I don't want to fight anymore," she confided, returning his kiss. "I want to call it quits with Ricky." She felt so fine, so damned fine. It was a wonderful new feeling. "I'll see him this morning. I'll tell him he can have his divorce."

Ed held her tight.

"We'll get married," he told her. "As soon as you're free, we'll get married."

She pressed her face against his chest.

"Oh, I'm so happy, Ed! For the first time I'm really happy."

He stroked her hair gently.

"I'm glad. For both of us."

They walked into the hall, his arm around her shoulders, her arm circling his waist.

"We'll build a marvelous camp together," Della said. "We'll have the best anywhere, won't we, Ed?"

"Sure."

"And we'll be happy. I know we will."

Together they went down the stairs, walking slowly, holding each other affectionately.

"It's like stumbling over a pot of gold," Ed stated. "With the kind of setting we have here we won't be able to miss. Give us a couple of years, just two or three, and we'll have enough money to last us the rest of our lives."

Della laughed, looking up at him.

"Oh, there isn't that much profit in it, Ed."

"You'll see," he said. "You'll see, dear."

Jennie was in the kitchen, seated on a high red stool at the counter, reading the previous Sunday's edition of a New York tabloid.

"It beats hell out of me," Jennie said, pushing the paper aside. "Those Hollywood dames try one guy after the other and they still can't find the right one. You'd think they'd wait until they got a divorce before they went and got engaged."

"Variety," Ed reminded her. "It's the spice of life."

Jennie got down from the stool, patting her middle.

"A girl can stand only so much variety," she said.

Della never had anything except coffee for breakfast but Ed wanted bacon and four eggs.

"Big day coming up," Ed said. "Bet we'll hit close to two hundred."

"Maybe Jennie'd better drive me into town, then."

Ed stood up from the table and winked down at her.

"Good luck," he said.

She smiled.

"I think I've already had my share," she told him soberly.

Della helped Jennie with the dishes and as soon as they were finished Jennie went upstairs and changed into a cool-looking green uniform.

"One thing I like about these uniforms," Jennie said, climbing into the car. "They'll stretch and stretch and stretch. And, believe me, that's what I need. Some thing with lots of stretch."

"Oh, you don't show any yet."

The station wagon rattled and banged as they steered it down the driveway.

"Well, it's already two months," Jennie observed. "And even if I don't show it, I feel it. But that's the way they say it happens most times. They say you go a long time and then all of a sudden you get up one morning and you look like you're gonna have an elephant the next second."

"Tell me about Sammy," Della said as they started down the mountain. "You haven't mentioned Sammy in a long time."

"I haven't been seeing Sammy, that's why."

"Oh?"

"No. Sammy's a little angry at me."

Della smiled and leaned back.

"Seems to me that your Sammy is angry at you most all of the time," she said.

The car slowed quickly.

"Look, Mrs. Farland, I hope you ain't gonna get angry at me too," Jennie began, "but—well, Sammy, didn't like it when I told him about that paper you had me sign. He said—sometimes I think Sammy is nuts. You know what he said? He said—well, maybe this isn't just the way he said it—but what he meant was that it was all right about the paper if something happened to me, the way you explained it. But supposing nothing did happen and it was a boy and it grew up to be a big shot, or something like that, and then Mr. Farland could—well, he could, you know—'

They rode a short distance in silence.

"You mean, Jennie, that Mr. Farland might take advantage of the boy because of the statement you'd signed?"

"I guess that's it, Mrs. Farland."

Della laughed.

"But I have the paper, Jennie. Mr. Farland doesn't have it."

"Honest, I don't know," Jennie said in desperation. "I signed that thing because you thought it was right and now Sammy says—"

"Your Sammy is a pretty smart boy, Jennie."

"Oh, you think so, Mrs. Farland?"

"Yes, I do."

Jennie let out a low whistle.

"Well, I'll be damned," she said. "I always thought Sammy was a little dense, to tell you the truth. Not that it's anything bad, mind you, because none of us can help it if we're like that, I always say."

The springs underneath the Ford walloped the frame as they went over the railroad tracks, and Della jerked upright.

"I can't promise you anything," Della said. "But you might get that paper back, after a while."

Jennie's eyes grew large.

"Honest?"

"Yes. If Mr. Farland is reasonable, And I think he will be. We'll know in a little while."

"Oh, so that's where we're going, is it?"

"Yes."

"I'm glad," Jennie said. "The more I think about it, the more I think that Sammy is right." She concentrated on her driving and soon they were in town. "Where you want to go, Mrs. Farland?"

"The railroad station. I'll use the phone."

Jennie let her off at the station and Della told the girl that she'd meet her later at the Breakers, a small commercial hotel further uptown.

"It's all right if I wait in the bar?" Jennie wanted to know.

"Sure. Knock yourself out."

The station in North Landing was typical Erie. It wasn't clean and it wasn't dirty. It wasn't really old and it wasn't very new. It was just a roof with a bunch of seats underneath. Della went inside and over to the phone booth.

She tried calling the Andersons first, thinking that they would know where she could reach Ricky. The doctor answered the phone and when he found out it was Della he snickered a little and said:

"So you're having quite a ball out there, hey? From what I hear—"

"Have you seen Ricky?" Della interrupted.

"Why, of course I've seen him."

"I mean, do you know where I can reach him?"

There was a moment's silence.

"Well, now, that's another thing. He was staying at the Breakers but I understand—well, it doesn't matter very much. He isn't there any longer."

"Then you don't know where he is?"

"Nope."

"Or is it that you wouldn't tell me if you did?"

"Certainly I'd tell you, Della." The doctor's voice lowered. "Hell, there's nothing wrong with what you're doing out there," he said, laughing. "It's just a bit shocking, that's all."

She hung up, her anger blazing. To hell with him, she thought. To hell with the whole damned bunch of them.

She tried the Breakers next but the man on the desk told her that Mr. Farland had checked out and that he didn't know where he could be reached. The man sounded glad that Mr. Farland wasn't with them any longer.

Next, she tried Dr. Berringer's office. The girl who answered said she didn't even know Mr. Farland, and was he a patient and should she have him call somebody if he came in. She dialled the Berringer residence last and Sally's voice came to her quickly.

"Sally, this is Della."

The wires hummed steadily.

"Yes, Della. What can I do for you?"

There was no hate in Sally's tone. No feeling. No nothing.

"I wanted to get in touch with Ricky," Della said, "I—I thought you might be able to help me."

"I haven't seen Ricky since day before yesterday," Sally said quietly.

"Oh?"

"No." Then, her voice rising, "Della, why did you do it? Why did you have to be so terrible and awful and mean?" She was close to hysteria. "You've brought me nothing but trouble, Della. Trouble. First, you took Ricky but that didn't satisfy you. You—you're not human, Della. You're not!"

"I'm sorry," Della said, meaning it. "Believe me, I'm very sorry. But things will be better now, Sally. You'll see, They'll be a lot better if—if I can only talk to Ricky."

"I'm not sure where he is," Sally said. "After last Saturday—well, it was perfectly awful, Della. He was at the Breakers and he got drunk—stinking drunk. I tried to talk to him but he wouldn't listen to me. He kept saying you were a bitch, a no-good bitch—but of course he was right. You know he was right, Della. Only he was so drunk—disgusting—and the man down there called me, but I wasn't home and he talked to Daddy. It was frightful!"

So now you've had it, Della thought. You've been a witness to Ricky Farland in action. She couldn't feel sorry for Sally.

"Tell me where I can find him," she said.

The wires hummed again.

"He was at the Clover Motel last night," Sally an swered finally. "But I let him know I wouldn't have. anything to do with him, wouldn't talk to him again, unless he came right over here and apologized to Daddy."

Della couldn't help laughing. Ricky apologize? That was a good one. Ricky wouldn't apologize to his mother if he ran over her with a truck.

"I'll try there," Della said and hung up.

She found the number of the Clover Motel in the directory and dialed.

Yes, Mr. Farland was a guest at the motel. Did she wish him called to the phone? No, he hadn't gone out; his car was still in front, and, as far as the woman knew, Mr. Farland was still sleeping. Very well, she would tell Mr. Farland that his wife had called and that she would be out in a few minutes.

Della left the station and hailed a cab outside. The driver was a hump-backed little man who had occasionally driven her up to Raven's Nest in the past.

"They say there's a lot of traffic up your road these days," he said, swinging the yellow DeSoto into the main street.

To hell with you, Della thought. To hell with you and all the rest of them with narrow, dirty minds. Together, she and Ed would show them. They'd show the people in the Landing that a nudist camp could be a highly respectable and worthwhile venture. And they' show Ricky Farland something very special. They'd show him what real love could mean, what it could accomplish.

"Hot, isn't it?" the driver wanted to know.

They rode a few minutes in silence, the tires of the cab hissing on the blacktop, the lush green fields of the countryside sliding past.

The driver's eyes regarded her soberly in the mirror.

"Sorry if I offended you, Mrs. Farland."

"That's all right."

"But you know how it is, some people can kid about things like that and some can't."

"I suppose so."

"I guess you don't feel that way about it."

"No," Della agreed. "I'm sure I don't."

They pulled in at the motel, a rambling green and white structure against a high pine-studded hill, and Della got out.

"Wait for me," she said.

The driver grinned, his eyes fastened on the top of her dress.

"Don't worry," he assured her. "I ain't been paid yet."

She turned and walked away, toward the green Caddy convertible parked close to one of the units. Looking at the car brought back memories of the day Ricky had bought it.

She went up to the door and knocked. A car with a loud muffler buzzed up the highway and backed off as it started down the next hill. A television unit in one of the rooms emitted the tragic details of a soap opera and from an open window, farther down, sounds of a woman's laughter emerged and drifted away. Della knocked again, louder and longer.

"Hey!" Ricky shouted. "What the hell, I'm not up yet."

"Ricky, open the door. It's Della."

She heard his feet moving across the floor.

"Hello, baby," he said and opened the door.

He wore only shorts, a white pair she had bought him on one of her trips to Newark.

"Hello," he said again.

She smiled and stepped into the room.

"Hi," she told him.

Both rear windows were open wide but the room still smelled like someone had washed the bed linen in a mixture of rye and gin. A few bottles, in various stages of use, stood on the dresser and a broken glass lay near one of the chairs.

"I refuse to apologize," Ricky said, closing the door. "You should have had a pretty good idea what it would look like, anyway."

He walked to the dresser and inspected one of the bottles.

"Drink?"

She shook her head.

"This calls for a celebration," he said, filling a shot glass. "You coming to see me, I thought the old pot had lost her mind when she gave me the word."

"I had to see you, Ricky," Della said.

He grinned at her and lifted the glass,

"Obviously."

She sat down in one of the chairs, watching him. He was good-looking, she thought, in a male, don't give a damn my pants aren't pressed way. His blond hair was more rumpled than usual and he had needed a haircut worse than ever.

"Could have gotten dressed," he said, lighting a cigarette. "But, cripes, I thought, what's the use of going to all that bother. In the first place, you're my wife. I've got nothing to hide that you don't know about already and, besides, since you run around in your skin half the time a little bare flesh, more or less, shouldn't bother you."

"Please, Ricky. I didn't come here to argue."

He breathed deeply of the smoke. He had a good body, she thought; wide, powerful shoulders. She had seen those innocent looking fists of his ball up and almost crush a man in Iceland with two wallops.

"So what did you come here for?" he wanted to know. "To gloat?"

"No. I came to talk to you about the divorce."

"I see."

"I—I won't stand in your way, Ricky. You can have the divorce."

He was quiet for such a long time that she thought he hadn't understood her. Then, filling the shot glass again, he smiled.

"Things have changed, is that it?"

"Yes," she admitted.

"In fact," he asked her, "now you'd even like the divorce, wouldn't you?"

"Yes."

"Because of that Loring fellow?"

"Yes." Somehow, she couldn't look at Ricky. "Ed Loring. I'm in love with him."

"And he's in love with you?"

"I'm sorry, Ricky."

"Sorry?" He laughed and slammed the glass down onto the dresser. "Hell, you're not sorry and you know it. And neither am I. You go your way and I go mine. What could be better?"

She stirred uneasily. There was something about Ricky that was different, unreal. His voice? The way he looked at her? She didn't know. She just knew that she almost wished that she hadn't come, that she had talked with him by telephone.

"It's the only way," she said.

He walked over to the bed and sat down, pushing his feet into his slippers.

"I'll tell you a shocker, Della. I'm sorry as hell for having taken a poke at you Saturday." His eyes studied her. "You may think that's a lot of crap, but it's the truth." He stood up again. "Hell, yes, I was mad at you, same as you were mad at me, but—well, I guess you must have known it, without me saying so, otherwise you wouldn't be here."

"Forget it," she said.

"That was a cute trick you pulled on me with that Jennie, you know. A guy can't buck something like that, baby. Even if a guy wins in court he's still finished."

"Yes."

"Whether it's true or not."

"I hope you're not denying it, Ricky."

She wished that she could shrink into the chair, crawl away, as he came and stood over her. He looked so big, so strong, and a bitter sneer pulled his mouth out of shape.

"Did you come here to talk about who's the father of Jennie's kid?"

"No."

"Or about us?"

"The divorce," she said hurriedly. "I wanted to tell you it was all right."

"Then leave Jennie out of it," he said.

She got up and he didn't stop her. She felt better when she was on her feet. She didn't feel so helpless.

"I just thought you'd like to know that it would never cause you any trouble," she explained. "I'll give the paper to Jennie and she can destroy it."

"Why not give it to me," he wanted to know, "and let me destroy it?"

"I don't know why not. I guess so."

"Then that's that," he said, returning to the dresser. This time he mixed the drink with a little water. "Now, let's see. I get the divorce, right?"

"Yes."

He stared at her for a long time.

"And what else?"

"I'd like a small drink," she said, suddenly nervous. "Just a tiny one."

"All right." He didn't bother to see if the glass was clean or not. "I asked you what else."

"There's nothing else," she told him lamely. "I have nothing to say."

He handed her the drink, his eyes never leaving her face.

"Well, I have plenty to say. I'll tune you in," He told her softly. "I'll bring you up with the news, baby. When I met you in Iceland, what were you?"

Some of the drink spilled down the front of her dress and he laughed as she glanced toward the door.

"Don't worry about it," he advised. "It's locked. You're going to listen to everything I've got to say be fore you leave, baby. And you ought to listen real good because I'm going to give it to you straight. First, I'll tell you what you were when you met me. You were a stateside hungry girl who'd give yourself to the first guy willing to get you a passport."

"Ricky!"

"Oh, I'm not blaming you. I'm just telling you. Hell, if I'd have been you I'd have done the same thing. I don't know why not. Who would want to spend the rest of his life on that stinking island?"

"Ricky," she said again. "Ricky, I'm trying to do what you want. I'm not fighting you."

"What do you mean you're not?" he demanded angrily. "You mean when you've had enough you think I've had enough, too, and that I ought to quit. You've been fighting me plenty, baby. You started it the day you went to the lawyer's. Sure, you foxed Tom Fielding because the stupid so-and-so didn't know any better. But you did something else, too, baby. Christ, I told you about that store, didn't I? I told you that I didn't have the money, didn't I? God damn it, what do you think we've been using for money since we've been married?"

She wished she could leave. She wished she had never come,

"Don't shout, Ricky."

"Don't shout," he sneered, moving around the room. "Don't shout, she says. Well, I will shout. And you know why? I'll tell you why. You know what they say in town? They say Ricky Farland married a whore and that she took him for his money and kicked him out. They don't think I wasted it, baby. They think I'm smart, most of them do, the way my old man was smart. They don't believe I went through it all because most of them think 'all' is ten times more than it was in the first place. No, they don't think or believe those things. They just think I was took by a designing woman."

"Maybe you were," she admitted quietly, determined to fight back, struggling to keep her voice level.

"Even my sister thinks so," he went on, ignoring her. "She knows I inherited the company and she thinks I'm a liar when I say the business wasn't worth a dime. Oh, sure, she was glad enough to come out and drink my liquor and eat my food, but when it came time for me to ask her for a buck you'd have thought I was a stranger."

Outside, the cars drummed up the highway, streaming northward. It was only Thursday but the weekend traffic had already begun.

"You tore it the other day," Ricky said. "You tore it good, baby. When I left the house I was so desperate I had to have a jug. So I got a jug. And I got drunk. I got so miserably drunk and I got so broke that Sally had to bail me out of the hotel. By that time everybody in town was talking about your paradise under the trees. Some of them said, 'Ricky, you old woman-chaser you, how do you get next to some of that stuff?' and some of them said, 'Ricky, it isn't any of my business but if your father was only alive—' It's the it-isn't-any-of-my-business boys that slay you, baby. They're the people who run the banks—the lawyers and the doctors—and everybody else who can make you or break you in a small town. They're people like Sally's old man and, I guess, Sally herself. They .get down on you for something like that—for crossing the moral line, they call it—and you might just as well slit your throat and let your blood run out."

Ricky poured another pair of drinks,

"I'll give you a handful of roses for one thing, though," he said. "When you slapped it to me, baby, you slapped it to me good. Even the day I left the house, knowing what I knew, I didn't believe it could be so bad." He looked down at his hands, shaking his head. "But a man learns. A man learns and then, sometimes, he changes."

"I'm honestly sorry," Della told him. She felt more certain of herself now that he had given her an opportunity to understand his resentment. "I was wrong, Ricky. If we couldn't get along, we couldn't get along. You were good to me in a lot of ways."

"Thanks for nothing."

"But I mean it, Ricky! And you're wrong about that states-hungry bit. I married you because I loved you—or thought I did."

"Nuts!" He went over to the bed and lay down, stretching out to his full-length. He folded his arms and placed them behind his head, staring up at the ceiling. "I'm not going to keep you much longer," he said. "And I'm not going to hit you. As soon as I'm finished you can leave. The door, by the way, isn't locked. I left it unlocked because I didn't know what I might do when I saw you. I think I hate you, Della. But I don't want to kill you."

"You don't have to say any more, Ricky."

"But I do, baby. I do. I have to tell you a very funny story. Remember when we left Iceland, how good it seemed, how happy we were? At least, I was happy."

"Yes." It was barely a whisper.

"And remember it was at night when we flew past the southern tip of Greenland? And the sky was all red fire and the clouds below were white and the hostess was sore because it was the first flight in two years that she hadn't brought along color film for her camera?"

"Yes, Ricky." She sank into the chair, remembering. "It's almost like yesterday."

"It was yesterday," he reminded her. "But I'll never forget it because it was the happiest day of my life. I wanted to tell you—but the sunset interrupted me and I never found the words again."

"I'd rather not talk about it now."

He rolled his head from side to side,

"You're right," he said. "It wouldn't do any good. No good at all."

"That was yesterday," she reminded him.

"Sure. Yesterday. Or maybe the day before yesterday."

The room got very quiet and outside a horn honked impatiently.

"Coming back to the divorce," Ricky said finally. "I told you I wanted something. I wasn't kidding., I do. I want the one thing that I should have kept and the one thing that doesn't belong to you. Baby, I want a clear title to the property at Raven's Nest."

Della sat there, stunned, unable to speak, unable to move.

"And I'm going to have it," Ricky promised solemnly. "I'm going to have it if I have to hang your filthy linen from the windows of every house between North Land ing and Keflavik."

Slowly, she arose from the chair. She could feel her heart leaping against her breast, pounding in her eyes. Her legs were weak and heavy.

"It's all I have, Ricky," she protested. "There's nothing else."

He waved her aside.

"You're forgetting about the stunt you played on my lawyer, aren't you? You're forgetting that you could have given me an easy divorce and you'd have had the place. And you're forgetting something else, too. You're forgetting that I've gotten myself in bad all around town and that this is the only way I can get out of it. The place means money to me, baby. And money means tomorrow. I'm betting all the way through on this one, baby. All the way or nothing at all."

"Ricky—"

He sat up quickly.

"I've told you what I want," he reminded her. "There's nothing else to say. Do I get it or don't I?"

She closed her eyes, thinking of Ed and of the plans they had made together. But she thought of something else, too, something that gave her the inward strength to open her eyes and smile at Ricky.

"All right," she whispered. "I'll take the trade."

Ed and she could always go somewhere else, she thought; they could always start again. As long as they were together, as long as they loved each other, nothing else was of great importance. Raven's Nest was nice but it wasn't the only place in the world. If this was the price Ricky demanded, then it was the price she would have to pay. She didn't want any messy court trials or fighting or anything like that. All she wanted was to settle matters once and for all, one way or the other. Sometimes, she knew, a person had to lose before they could gain.

"This Ed Loring must be quite a guy," Ricky said.

She looked straight at him. "He is." She went to the door and it opened under her touch.

"I'll have the papers drawn up in the next couple of days," Ricky said. "And don't try going back on your word about it, this time."

"Don't worry. I won't."

His lips twisted into a smile. "A person would almost think that you want to get rid of me."

"You don't know how much!"

She turned, happy that it was over at last, and left.

Ricky's laughter followed her all the way out to the waiting taxi.

10

DANK CLOUDS ROLLED low over the mountains and flashes of lightning ripped through the sky. Thunder boomed through the valleys and across the highlands, shaking the late afternoon with spasmodic, heavy crashes. Outside, a windswept rain began to fall in torrents.

Della stood at the window watching Ed Loring coming up the lane toward the house; his head lowered against the storm. In one hand he clutched the remains of a once-good umbrella and just as he reached the porch he threw it away.

"Hey!" he yelled, entering the kitchen. "Anybody here?"

"In the living room, Ed."

"Man, but it's really pouring!" He came through the archway, pushing the wet hair up from his forehead. "You just get back?"

"A little while ago."

He fumbled in his shirt, looking for cigarettes.

"Wet," he said, disgustedly.

"There are some on the table."

He found the pack of Winstons and lit one.

"You see your husband?"

"Yes."

Ed sighed and sat down on the couch and a puddle of water began to form on the rug.

"How'd you make out?"

She walked around the room, trying to think, trying to find the words with which to answer. For a few moments after she'd left Ricky she had felt so sure, so positive that she was doing the right thing. But on the way home, as she had driven along in the car, the old fear had come back—the fear that Ricky had never been able to understand. And no one, she thought now, not even Ed, would ever be able to understand it, this anxiety that churned within her. Not unless they had been raised on an island where the summer air was filled with the stink of drying codfish, not unless they knew what it was like to pay a week's wages for a pair of nylon stockings or a day's salary for a package of American cigarettes. And they would have had to live along the sea wall and hear the angry waves of the North Atlantic pounding upon the door every night, to have had their father go to sea on one of the whalers and never come back. They'd have had to have a mother die of tuberculosis because the winter nights were so endless and the food was so terrible and money was so scarce.

Or they would have to have been fourteen as she had been fourteen—and given a jar of peanut butter, only to listen to the hilarious laughter of the Americans afterwards, when she'd taken it out of the oven nicely baked, simply because she'd been so ignorant that she hadn't known any better. They'd have had to live in a country where the male of the species could own you for a night or a day or a week or a month where you got on a darkened bus and, quite suddenly, found an American's hand under your dress, like you were a tramp or a whore or a public sex-machine. No, not until a person had known such things, not until they had struggled with and mastered the strange phrases of the English language, could he know why those from the island had to be able to see what they owned, had to be able to touch it with possessive care and be sure, deep down inside, that it would always be there and always belong to them.

This wasn't, Della knew, just a part of her life, this desire, this constant yearning for security, this almost fanatic urge to know that the future would be sound and safe. It was, she knew, all of life.

"Ed," she heard herself saying, not listening to the thunder, not seeing the lightning flashes over the lake. "Ed, Ricky says I have to turn this place over to him or he won't give me a divorce." She could feel the tightening of her throat, feel the rising panic in her voice. "Ed, I didn't want to. I didn't! But there was no other way. None. It's for us, Ed. And it has to be right because it's for us."

Ed returned to the table and very carefully picked up another cigarette.

"I thought it was the other way around," he said slowly. "I thought you were giving him something."

"Ricky's changed."

"It would seem so," Ed said.

"He's—desperate. That's what I think. I think he's so far down that he'll move heaven and earth to get this property away from me. I'm sure he'll fight me, Ed. I know he will. And, anyway, a court would probably say that I had backed down on my word, that I had done the wrong thing."

"I thought you never signed anything."

"I didn't. It was just an understanding."

Ed put down the cigarette and came over to her. He put his arms around her and kissed her on the mouth.

"Then what are you worrying about? Just tell him to go to hell."

She shook her head.

"I can't, Ed. I can't. Don't you see? Maybe it would be best to give him what he wants—so that we could be together and I wouldn't have to fight with him any more. Isn't it worth giving up something, Ed, so that we can be happy?"

The wetness of his clothes seeped through her dress, touching her skin. She felt herself shiver.

"What about the camp?"

"He'd never let it stay, once he had the place in his hands. You know that."

Ed kissed her on the forehead. Her lips pressed against his wet shirt, moved away.

"But he doesn't have anything to say about it. Not yet."

"We'll find another place," she told him confidently. "You'll see. We'll find a place that will beat Raven's Nest all hollow!"

"Not easily, we won't."

"Well, one just as good."

"I doubt it."

"Or you can go into advertising," Della said. "Isn't that what you used to do? You can get a job in advertising and we can get a little apartment somewhere. I've still got a few dollars left. Not much, but enough to get furniture and things. And we've got the station wagon. It isn't as though we didn't have anything or were stone broke."

"Della," he said.

"We aren't losing everything," she insisted, holding him tight. "We aren't losing anything at all, we'll have each other, won't we? We don't need any more than that. We'll never need more than that!"

"Della."

She felt his body tense, his strong brown hands seeking her arms, shoving them aside.

"Della," he said again, facing her.

Something earnest and powerful crowded up into his dark eyes, washing over her.

"This isn't kid stuff," he said bluntly. "This camp is big business, Della."

"I know that, Ed."

"But you don't. You don't know the first thing about it. All you know is that you earned a couple of hundred bucks last week. Right?"

She nodded. Two hundred and eighteen dollars and seventy-five cents, to be exact.

"That's peanuts," Ed said. He went to the table and picked up another cigarette. "Peanuts."

"I only want to do what's right for us," Della said.

"And what about the people?" Ed demanded. "The Holdens. And the rest of them. The ones I dragged up here!"

"Things have changed."

"Have they?" He shook his head. "Not that much, they haven't."

"But, Ed—"

"You want me to go down there and tell them to get out? You want me to tell Arch Holden that this has been just a one-week stand?"

"Ed, we have to! There's no other way. Ricky—"

"Ricky this and Ricky that!" he said irritably. "Stop thinking about that guy for a minute, won't you? Get interested in me and some of the others who have put money in your pocket."

"I am interested in you," Della said truthfully. "I'm in love with you, Ed."

"You're not showing it."

"But I am, Ed. I am!"

"Then, don't go around throwing a lot of money down the drain." He flung his cigarette into the fireplace. "Hell, do you know how hard it is to find a spot like this, Della? Of course you don't. You don't know because you never looked for one. But I have and I know. And I know where money can be made. Right here. In less than two years we can walk out with a bundle. Just remember that."

She moved toward him, breathing deeply, her legs heavy.

"I think you're forgetting that I put up quite a bit of money, Ed. I'll lose most of that and I know it."

He stared at her.

"For someone who's almost as flat as rain on a roof you're sure careless with a dollar," he said.

She stopped very still, looking at him.

"Ed," she said lamely. "Ed, tell me—"

"Tell you what?"

"That it's all right—between us, I mean."

"It is if you stick with this place, Della."

Suddenly she had to know, had to be sure. Those moments that she remembered, moments of unrestrained passion and tender promises, were no longer enough. There had to be something more, something deeper.

"Ed, do you love me?"

His glance was thoughtful.

"Physically, you mean?"

"No. Not just that."

"I don't know of any other way," he said. "If there is one."

He might as well have slapped her across the face. It hurt that much. "Oh, Ed!"

"It's time you stopped being a kid," he told her savagely. "And it's time we both stopped playing games. You might just as well know right now, Della, that you're not going to turn this property over to your husband and that we're not going to get out."

She looked away from him, her breath choking against the ball of pain in her chest.

"I'd hoped that everything would go smoothly and you wouldn't have to know the hard facts," he told her. "But I guess it isn't going to be that way. You had to go and louse things up with this deal with your husband."

Della gasped. She couldn't believe her ears.

"This is a big game we're playing here, Della. For big stakes. Remember those pictures of Ken's that you found?"

Della nodded mutely.

"Nothing wrong with them?"

She shook her head.

"But suppose a person didn't want them taken? Suppose you have a guest who is worth a lot of money, or has a good job, and doesn't want his picture taken—but you take it anyway? What then? It's worth money, isn't it? I mean, to the person in the picture, if he can buy the prints and the negatives."

"That's blackmail!"

"No, it isn't. You wouldn't say a girl who takes pictures in a night club was a blackmailer, would you?"

"Oh, Ed!"

She stared at him, shocked, trying to reconcile him with the man who had made love to her. The man she had permitted to know every secret glory of her body. She couldn't reconcile anything. He was gone, washed away the way the dust had been washed away by the rain. She began to cry.

"I'm telling you all this because I want you to know the worst of it, right now," he said. "Once you're a part of it and once you know you're a part of it I think you'll see things in a different light."

"You never cared," Della whispered, almost to herself. "I never meant anything to you."

He grinned at her.

"But you did."

"You don't act as though I did."

"All right," he said simply. "You meant—and still mean—exactly this. You're one of the best girls I ever had—and about the easiest. You take it from there."

She went over to him and slapped him hard across the face. He laughed and she slapped him again.

"I've been a fool," she moaned.

Outside, the storm had drifted away and the sun had emerged. A clean damp breeze blew up from the lake, rattling the venetian blinds.

"I believe you'll be happier if you don't do that again," Ed was saying. "In fact, if you just settle down, continue taking in money the way you have been, and keep that pretty little mouth of yours shut, you might even get to be real happy."

Della's temper mounted, blazing furiously.

"Get out of here!"

"Now is that any way to talk?" He was laughing at her. "Maybe you wouldn't make the same deal with me again, but you made it and you're stuck with it. At first, I thought you were just a little stupid but, hell, this nudist thing was right up your alley. In a way, being an Icelander you were used to nudity and you had none of the reservations that an American girl might have had."

"But blackmail!" she returned heatedly. "That has no place in this at all, Ed. Not for me. And you know it as well as I do."

Again he laughed at her.

"Get one thing straight," he said. "We're in this to clean up a fat profit, and you can't do that with nudist camps if you run them according to the book. Oh, some do all right when they get around to taking casuals or when they let all the barriers down so that certain types of girls and boys can have a ball. But that's petty stuff and before long you have the cops on your neck. Our operation is different. We sell the pictures to the people if they want them and if they don't want them, they can just keep on wondering what we might do with them. It's all pretty simple, really."

How could it have happened, she asked herself? He'd been a stranger, a man she liked, and now he had plunged her into something that seemed so dirty. Ed, she supposed, was right. She had been easy. It was like cutting yourself with a razor blade; you couldn't believe a little thing like that could do such big damage.

"We might even put on some parties at the camp," Ed was saying. "You know, discreet little affairs at which those who enjoy such things could have some fun."

"I'm not interested."

"Well, I can make you interested. You're the land owner. If things get a bit out of line and the law hears about it, you might be construed an accessory."

Her eyes flashed. "Are you threatening me?"

"I'm just saying the cops could be tipped off. They'd make trouble for you."

"Not if I got to them first, they wouldn't."

"But you're not going to them. First. Or last."

A blind, breathless fury flooded through her. She felt herself moving to the telephone, felt her hand lift the receiver, her finger searching for the dial.

"I don't want to do this," she said huskily. "But I have to."

Ed came and stood beside her. She could see him smiling, shaking his head. He placed something in her hand.

"Go ahead," he said. "But you'll have trouble explaining this."

Her glance lowered, slowly. Her eyes found the photo, lingered for an agonizing moment and then her sight blurred, refusing to accept what she saw. From way down inside, so deep that it seemed to be past any human limits, she screamed just once.

"I think you're inclined to agree with me," Ed said calmly.

Her stare returned to the photo, drawn there as though by some hideous but irresistible force.

"Oh, God!"

"Of course, you didn't pose for this nude picture," he admitted. "I know that and so do you. But do you want it circulated?"

She wished that tears would come, that they would blind her forever.

"Filth!" She shuddered. Then, "Ed, how could your"

"It was easy," he told her. "Nothing to it. Ken sneaked a shot through a peephole in the dressing tent."

"And I suppose that's how you make those pictures you—you sell?"

"Sometimes. Not always."

"How could you do this to anyone?" She crumpled the picture in her tiny fist. "How could you?"

"Go ahead. Tear it up. We have more prints," he said.

She got up and walked away from him; her mouth, her hands, and every part of her body felt numb.

"I may have seemed easy to you," Della said. "And I guess I was. But I didn't deserve this."

"It's the only protection we have."

"I see."

"And definitely you were easy."

She took a deep breath, facing him.

"All right. Ricky will fight me," she reminded him. "He'll fight me every inch of the way for this property."

"I doubt it," Ed said. "We had you both figured in on this, you know. We have to stay here at least until fall. Hell, it's too late in the season to go moving around. So we put Ada onto your husband. It wasn't hard, you might like to know. She just walked up to a bar, sat down next to him. That's all there was to it."

Ada, she thought, Ada and Ricky. Yes, it would have been easy for Ada to tempt Ricky. Easy for any pretty girl.

"We've got to get this straightened out once and for all," Ed was saying. "The thing for you to do is get on the phone and tell that husband of yours to get out here tonight. Then we'll see what's what."

"No!"

"I'm telling you, Della, This is big stuff, a big weekend coming up and I'm not playing with fire. I want the fire out. Period."

She looked out of the window at the lake and the fields and the green hills beyond. It was such a lovely place, she thought. But people insisted on spoiling it.

"He won't come," she said. "I know he won't."

Ed pointed to the phone.

"Call him."

God, she thought, she had to think this over. She was going at it all wrong. She had to figure out what she should do and just how to do it.

"Call him, I said!"

She walked over to the phone book and found the number of the motel. Dialling the number, she smiled at Ed. She had made up her mind. She would play it his way. All his way.

"I'm sorry, Ed," she said.

He lit a cigarette and watched her through the smoke.

"Well, that's better."

"Things moved too fast for me, I guess."

"Sure."

She gave Ricky's name to the woman who answered in the motel office.

"He'll be madder than hops," Della said.

Ed laughed and walked around the room.

"Hello." It was Ricky's voice, finally on the line, "Who's this?"

"Della."

"Oh"

"About that trade we talked about this afternoon, Ricky—well, I'd like to have you come out tonight, if you will. I'd like to go over it with you again."

"Changed your mind, huh?" His tone was cold, "I thought you would."

She glanced at Ed to see if he might have heard. She was pretty sure he hadn't.

"No," she said. "It isn't that. It's—something else."

There was a moment's silence,

"You sure?"

"We'll talk about it when you get here."

"All right," he said finally. "I'll try to make it."

Ricky, she thought as she hung up, we've been a couple of utter fools. Maybe there isn't anything between us, and maybe there never was anything, but we have to lick this one together. We really do.

"Okay?" Ed demanded.

She tossed her hair, blonde and full, and forced a laugh.

"Okay," she said.

This was the way to handle Ed, she thought. The only way that gave her any chance of coming out of it.

"But I still think you're a louse," she said, smiling again. "You could have told me before."

He stopped and stared at the rumpled picture.

"Hell, I don't know if I follow you," he said cautiously, dropping the picture into his shirt pocket. "A couple of minutes ago you were going to yell for the cops. Why the big switch?"

"I told you things moved too fast for me," she said, lighting a cigarette. "They did. I'm just a little Icelander, you know."

She came over close to him.

"It's all right, Ed," she told him. "No hard feelings."

His eyes moved from her face down over the curves of her body, drinking them in. She stood like a statue while he kissed her on the mouth.

"You're quite a girl," he said.

It was only after he was gone that she cried.

11

RICKY PHONED SHORTLY before seven. He said he had a flat on his car and that he hadn't been able to get it changed.

"Well, get a cab," she told him. "I'm waiting for you.

"She hoped he wouldn't want to put it off. She'd been thinking about this mess for hours and she knew that they had to do something about it quickly or it might be too late.

"No, you get somebody to drive you in," Ricky said.

"I'd rather not."

"Look," he said impatiently. "I've got to see you. And, Christ Almighty, I'm not going to walk out there, Della."

"Get a cab," she said again.

Jennie had borrowed the station wagon to drive down to the Landing to look for Sammy.

"And pay for it with what?" Ricky queried. Then, more gently, "Hell, I don't blame you for being sore. I guess I was a little hard on you today. I—I apologize, Della."

This was something new, she thought, Ricky apologizing.

"Go on."

"After you left I did some footwork and what I came up with doesn't look so good for you or me. What I found out about Raven's Nest—and I'm not blaming you, either—is big enough to cancel both of us out if we aren't damned careful."

He was talking now like the Ricky she had known in Iceland, a man who faced things as they came, with courage and energy.

"A lot of things have been happening," he continued. "You know this fellow Ed Loring? Well, he was a friend of Sally's, or Sally was a friend of his sister, I guess, and now she says I'm the one that put Ed Loring onto her. Can you tie that, for heaven's sake? How stupid can she get? Hell, I never saw the guy more than two or three times in my life."

"I guess that's true," Della said.

Ricky's laugh was short and sober.

"I told her to go to hell, that's what I told her. And her old man, he calls me, blazing mad, and I told him to drop dead. Then that brother-in-law of mine, I'm talking to him, and he says it's hurt his practice—this nudist stuff—and I tell the bastard he never had a practice to hurt."

Ricky was boiling mad, flooding with rage like a river gone wild.

"That's what I wanted to talk to you about, Della. That's why I've got to see you. This Loring guy is one of the biggest leeches who ever crawled up out of a sewer. It's time, baby, that you and I quit our fighting for a spell and try to lick this thing together. You there, baby?"

"Of course, I'm here."

Ricky, she thought, you fool Ricky, you must have sobered up at last.

"I'll cue you in on another thing," Ricky said. "There isn't much time. Saturday night is going to be their big night. They only need one sucker night to haul in a big fortune and the next day—if the cops come—you're apt to be there all by yourself with the evidence, enough evidence to send you to jail for ten years."

She had thought of that, too, this afternoon, after Ed had left. She had thought of prison and what it would be like. And her thoughts had gone beyond prison to something else, to the things they did to a person who killed another.

"This is our problem," Ricky told her. "It's up to us to lick it."

"You really feel that way?"

"I wouldn't say so if I didn't."

Her eyes grew moist.

"I'm glad, Ricky. Glad!"

She was. This was the way it should be. For the moment, she had to forget about Ricky's mistakes and he had to overlook some of hers. It was the only way they could crawl up over the edge.

"Get a cab and come down, Della."

She didn't hesitate. "Right away."

"We'll work this thing out. Don't you worry, baby."

They said goodbye and she hung up. A moment later she dialled the cab number at the railroad station. Yes, she was told, a cab could be out in a few minutes.

Hurriedly she ascended the stairs and walked into her bedroom. She slipped out of the shorts and halter, tossed them on the foot of 'the bed, got a pair of black panties from a dresser and stepped into them. She picked up a bra, threw it down again, and struggled into a pink, tight-fitting sweater. For a skirt she chose a white thing that hugged her middle and accentuated her hips. The white sandals were all right, she decided, so she left them on.

Back downstairs she turned out the light in the kitchen, locked the doors and went out on the front porch to wait.

Mid-evening shadows fell across the hills and the sounds of the night crept in through the trees. A whippoorwill cried for its mate and the answer came, moments later, from far away. A distant train whistle moaned twice and the shadows on the ground grew longer, darker.

It was a beautiful place, she thought. Beautiful. This wonderful house Ricky had built for her had been such a dream at first. She remembered when they used to drive up during the time the foundation was being poured, and how they would stand on the high mound of dirt, looking down into the ugly hole in the ground, planning the way they would place the furniture, the colors of paint they would use. She remembered, too, their first night in the house, just the two of them, and how Ricky carried her all the way upstairs. Beautiful. And then she remembered the empty bottles, the long hours of drinking and dancing, the curses that followed those hours and the slaps and the blows that came upon the heels of the curses. Beyond this she did not want to remember, because beyond this there was just now, this past week.

The cab arrived about eight, its headlights cutting a wide path through the heavy dusk.

"Hi," said the hunchbacked driver.

"Hi, yourself."

She got in, smiling, forcing herself to look carefree and placid.

"Take me to that motel," she told him. "Where I went this morning."

The driver put the car in gear and shook his head sadly.

"The way you cried after we left there I didn't think you'd ever go back again."

It was funny enough, she thought; he was right.

"People are nuts," Della informed the driver.

Part way down the mountain a car came up close behind them, its lights high and bright, then it dropped back and the lights lowered.

"Ain't seen Mr. Farland around in quite a while," the driver said. "He been away?"

"Sort of."

You little snoop, she thought, no wonder you've got a crooked back; somebody must have broken it for you. She settled back in the seat and thought about herself and Ricky. People were not only funny but also stubborn and foolish! Why hadn't she helped Ricky when he'd been hitting the booze? Why hadn't she tried to understand him a little better?

"You crying again?" the driver wanted to know.

"Noo."

Damn you, Ricky, she thought, damn you! Why did it have to be Jennie? Why did it have to be anybody at all? Damn you!

That ended it, she decided, if it wasn't ended already. She could forgive Ricky almost anything, but not that, not Jennie.

The cab rolled on down the highway and she closed her eyes. That Ed Loring, she thought bitterly, there was one guy who should have been born with four legs and a fur coat. And he had seemed so nice at first, so gentle. She laughed bitterly. It was a question as to whether he had been nice to her or she had been nice to him. The easiest, he'd said, one of the easiest he'd ever had. Well, he'd find out. He'd find out that he would have to pay a big price, after all.

"Almost there, Mrs. Farland."

"Fine," she said.

She felt dirty, unclean, both mentally and physically. Her hands passed down over her breasts, her hips. Was this the same skin that Ed Loring had touched? Was this the body she had given to him, the same body that she had wanted him to own? Her hands moved up to her face, the same face she had seen in the photograph. How low could a man get, to what depths could he go? And how could a woman—she broke off the thought and shook her head, disgusted with all mankind, including herself.

The cab stopped in front of the motel.

"Wait for you, Mrs. Farland?"

She gave him a five and got out. "Not tonight," she said.

He leered back at her. "Have fun."

She walked toward Ricky's unit. Well, she'd made the cab driver's night complete; he had something to talk about now. Just took Mrs. Farland down to the motel, he'd tell his friends. Took her down and she's gonna stay all night. And then they'd laugh knowingly.

There was no light in Ricky's room but the Caddy was still out front. The car sat level enough, she noticed. Not the way it should with a flat. She knocked on the door and it opened quickly.

"Come on in," Ricky invited.

She entered the darkened room. The door snapped shut behind her and then Ricky's figure moved away from her.

"I wondered if you'd come," he said.

She stepped forward and bumped into a chair.

"Why aren't the lights on, Ricky?"

He fumbled with something in the darkness.

"Be patient," he said.

A breeze came through one of the open windows, soft and gentle. It carried with it the odor of perfume, a heady thick smell that swept up into her nostrils.

"Ricky!"

Her voice broke like glass shattering. She stumbled again, turning to the door, her hand fumbling for the knob in the darkness.

"Save your strength," he told her. "This time it's locked."

She twisted the knob, jerking at the door, but it wouldn't move.

"You lied to me, Ricky!" Her voice rose. "This is a trick, a damned trick! Who's here with you?"

"Shut up!" Ricky said. "This isn't out at the Nest. We've got neighbors here, baby. And I don't want them disturbed."

She thought she saw something against the further wall, over the bed, like a sheet somehow hanging there.

"Ricky," she pleaded. "I came here in good faith. I—"

"Sit down," he advised her shortly. "Sit down, or what you're going to see will knock you down."

Della remained still, not moving, waiting. The odor of the perfume whirled around her again, stronger this time.

"But, Ricky—"

"Shut up! I know why you wanted to see me. You think I'm a fool? You wanted to back out of our little deal, didn't you? Well, you're not going to! Not this time. This time—"

"Oh, Ricky, no! I wasn't."

But then a square of light flashed over the bed, reflecting from the sheet. "Good evening, Mrs. Farland," Ada Holden said. She was behind a movie projector that rested on a night table. Her skin, in the shadows, was very white, her hair blacker than the clouds of night. "Shall I let it roll, Ricky?"

"Just a second," he said. He moved toward Della, his shoulders hulking, his hands way down at his sides. "Don't worry, I'm not going to hit you. After a preview of what you're going to see I wouldn't touch you with a tenfoot pole in somebody else's hand,"

Della leaned against the door, weak and frightened.

"Haven't you done enough, Ricky? Haven't we both done enough? Ricky—"

"Don't shout." His face loomed above her, very white.

"Just watch the show—if you can. When it's over I've got a little paper for you to sign. A transfer of the property back to me. And that's all. You don't have to do one other thing, baby. You sign that paper and we'll be shut of each other for keeps."

She didn't know what it was she was going to see, why he had asked her to come here or what he might do. She knew only one thing, knew it with every throbbing nerve within her. She would defy him. And she told him, clearly, bluntly, so there could be no misunderstanding.

"Go to hell, Ricky!"

For an instant she thought that he was going to strike her. Her body tensed, ready for it, waiting. But then he laughed, the whisky on his breath washing over her face.

"Show her the movie star, Ada," he said.

The light on the sheet faded, becoming gray. A few black lines appeared and slid into oblivion. The motor of the projector hummed steadily.

"I'm afraid the pictures aren't very good," Ada explained. "You see, the lighting wasn't the best at the time they were taken and even a topnotch photographer can only do so much. However," she continued, as the ridge pole of a tent came into view, "I believe you will easily recognize the scene, the characters and, I have no doubt, the action."

"Too bad there isn't any sound," Ricky said.

Ada laughed and laid her head against his shoulder.

The angle of the camera shifted suddenly, showing a pile of boxes against one side of the tent. Then it went up to the ridge pole, following that to the front of the tent, crossing the narrow opening in the flap, descending slowly,

"And there you are, baby," Ricky said softly.

There could be no doubt about it this time. There she was in the arms of Ed Loring, both of them naked, two people who owned four hands that had gone suddenly berserk.

"Just a couple of toys of a thing called sex," Ada described it. "Two happy people with nothing on their minds—or backs."

Della looked away, down at the dark floor, wishing that she could go somewhere and lie down on the ground and be sick, so sick that she'd die from it. Was there no limit to the vicious schemes people could devise? And Ricky, Ricky her husband, the man she had loved—where would it all end for him, for her, for all of them?

"Turn it off!" she whispered.

Ricky coughed.

"You've seen enough?"

She nodded and he repeated the question.

"Yes!" she shouted. "Yes, yes, yes! I've seen enough. Stop it!"

The projector droned on.

"Turn it off, Ada."

Ricky came across the room.

"You'll get the film after you've signed the paper," he told Della.

Her tears rolled soundlessly down her cheeks.

"I guess it was a rough way to do it," he admitted.

She wanted to scream at him, to call him every vile name, but she could not get a word out.

"I guess you've got nothing to say." He seemed almost unhappy that she hadn't fought against it, called it a lie.

Ada Holden laughed.

"That sure is one hell of a movie," she said.

Della clung to the door, her elbows tight against her sides. Then abruptly there was a sharp sound in the room, as though the sheet had been ripped into shreds. Della jerked up her head just as a light blazed from one of the windows, blinding her, filling the room with brightness. Ricky swore violently and the projector wavered precariously as Ada leaped to her feet.

"Say!" Ada demanded. "What do you think—"

The voice from the window was low, muffled. "Take the film out of that machine and hand it to me." Then, as Ricky took a step, "Don't anybody get wise. I've got a gun here and I'll put a hole through the first one who gives me any trouble."

Della tried to recognize the voice but she couldn't. It was strange and heavy, as though spoken by a big man. There was nothing hurried in the way the man spoke; he seemed confident enough. Only his hand poking through the window into the room, holding the flashlight steady, was visible. Beyond the hand there was nothing except the night.

Ricky stormed, "This is a hell of a note!"

"One of her men friends," Ada said, nodding at Della. "She must have a million."

The ball of light moved to Ada's face, held it in a gleaming white circle.

"I told you, lady. Give me the film."

Ada handed the twin reels to Ricky and, stiff-legged, he approached the window. The flashlight was withdrawn from the room, poised at a safe distance.

"Just put them through the hole, mister." Ricky did as he was told. "Now, go back to the bed and sit down." The hand with the light crept back inside, focusing once again upon Ada Holden. "You too, girlie."

The light lingered upon the bed. Ricky was wiping his face with a corner of one of the sheets and Ada's body seemed to swell inside her black dress, threatening to burst free.

"Mrs. Farland?"

"Yes."

"Unlock the door and go outside."

She didn't know what to expect out there but anything was better than being in this room.

"I haven't any key."

"Give it to her," the voice commanded Ricky.

Ricky threw the key and it landed on the floor. Della picked it up, unlocked the door.

"You can go now, the voice told Della. Addressing Ada and Ricky it was less gentle. "Don't try to follow her, either one of you. In fact, don't leave the room for an hour."

Della stepped out of the cabin, closing the door after her.

The night was clear and cool and a moon hung low over the tops of the trees. A milk tanker boomed up the highway, slowed at the hill as its gears ground. A couple of hot-rodders went by, motors churning, their straight-through Hollywood mufflers drowning out the sound of the truck.

Della walked across the yard, the shale crunching under her feet. She came to the end of the long line of darkened cars and lighted windows. When she reached the office she turned to enter, intending to call a taxi.

A car, running without lights, drifted across the parking lot. It came alongside her and stopped.

"Get in," the driver said.

It was Ed Loring.

"I'm not that crazy," Della said.

"I know what you're thinking," he said earnestly. "You've got it figured that I had that movie taken of us, haven't you? Well, you're way out in left field on that one. I didn't know Ken had a camera on. us. If I had known, I'd have killed the bastard right there."

Della swung away from the car.

"Look," Ed persisted. "I didn't come here to bring those pictures. I came to take them back. They're right here on the front seat."

Della turned and faced him, her eyes wide.

"Ed ... then, that was you!"

He laughed. "The man in the window."

"Oh, Ed!"

Sure, she hated him, she told herself. He was a human hog and worse than that, but what he had just done wiped out a lot of the past.

She ran to the car, half crying, half sobbing.

"Ed, I can't thank you enough!"

He reached across the seat and opened the door.

"Come around and get in. We've got to get out of here."

She did as she was told.

"But your voice," she said as they swung out of the driveway. "It sounded so different."

"Lucky I learned something in a school play once," he told her, peaking the motor before letting it drop into high. "I was supposed to be a ship's captain, talking off stage, and I disguised my voice by talking into a water glass. Only thing I ever learned in school that did me any good. But maybe it's a big dividend. That bitch Ada would have me out hunting a headstone if she knew."

They drove for a while in silence.

"Funny thing," Ed said finally. "When that cab came up to the house and you went out alone I thought you were up to something. That's why I followed you."

She remembered the car that had trailed them down the mountain.

"So you've been watching me," she said.

He shook his head.

"No, I was on my way up to the house. I tried the kitchen door, found it locked, and then saw this cab. When that happened I just grabbed the first car with a key in it and took off."

"And the gun?"

He swung off the highway and the big car swept up the hill road.

"Hell, I didn't have any gun. A bluff, that's all."

He's not afraid, she thought, not afraid of anything. He's like an animal that way. And in other ways.

"First thing we do is burn the film," he said.

"Thank the Lord for that!" Della sighed and leaned back against the cushion. "What a sucker I was to go down and meet Ricky."

"It's better this way," Ed reasoned. "At least, we've got the film and we know where it is. And you're under no illusions about that husband of yours."

"Yes, that's all true."

She rolled down the window and let the night air rush in against her. Ricky had played his big hand and lost everything, including his thumb and fingers. She was thoroughly finished with him.

"I thank you again." She breathed deeply. "Very much."

"This play with your husband tonight stumps me," he said. "You see, Arch thought, being that you two were separated, that it might cause trouble, That's why Ada's been working on Ricky, though my guess is that she wasn't supposed to go so far. Unless—unless—"

"Unless what?"

His hands tightened on the wheel and the car swayed.

"Unless they're trying to take me," he explained. Then he rushed on, excitedly, "Yeah, that must be it! If you'd have signed that transfer title I'd have been out. Don't you see? Their only hold on the place has been through me, because of you. Take you out and I'm out. Put your husband in and they're in. Simple, isn't it?"

"I don't know. I just can't picture Ricky—"

"He needs money, doesn't he?"

"Well, yes, but—"

"And it wouldn't be just that," Ed said knowingly. "It would be more than that, with Ada working on him. She'd get him drunk—that wouldn't be very hard, would it? And then—"

"Please," Della said. "Let's not talk about it."

They rode a short distance in silence.

"I can't see why they'd want to cut you out," Della said finally. "You've done a lot for the Holdens, haven't you?"

He nodded, lighting a cigarette, the flare of the match outlining his face.

"It's the girl," he said. "That Ada. She hates me."

"I wouldn't have thought so."

Ed shrugged and dimmed his lights for an approaching car.

"If you want to know, I threw in with the Holdens three years ago because I thought I was in love with Ada. It was like being in love with a stick of wood, something that wasn't even alive. But I held on, thinking that it would be different, hoping that it would change. But all that happened was that she came to resent me. She's jealous of everything I do for the Holdens. She regards me as a rival, an interloper. She feels I have too much influence—"

Ed's foot pressed the gas pedal, and the car roared up the mountain.

12

FRIDAY WAS A busy day. The horde of sun lovers began to arrive shortly before noon, in Caddys and Chryslers and other big cars of the carriage trade. The parking lot behind the house overflowed and spilled down across the field, almost to the lake.

"Look at 'em," Ed said once. "Just look at 'em!"

Men and women. Old and young. Many of them important people with low numbers on their license plates and four-figure amounts on their paychecks. All crawling up in the mountain to live it up under the sun. On Monday they would be back at their desks, or in their fancy homes, and the hunger would be satisfied for a little while, only to appear again a few days later.

"There's something to this nudist thing," Della said.

She realized that a deep and earnest yearning for freedom and health was what drove these people to the camp. And they came, she knew, because they considered the camp the real thing. A legitimate, moral establishment where they could pursue their hobby in peace and in privacy.

"You have to get them to feel that the place is safe," Ed had told her. "Take a banker, for instance, you have to sell him on the idea that once he goes on the reservation his identity is lost. You have to assure him that his participation will never plague him in his business life. Can you imagine what it would do to a bank president if it got around that he was a nudist?"

Della watched them come, smiling men and pleasant-faced women. Happy couples, mostly. And plenty of children. Ada Holden stopped at the house once during the day but she gave no indication that she was even remotely aware of the incident of the night before,

"She's a sharp one," Ed said after she'd left. "She'll play this all the way out to the end, though she's lost that reel of film."

"You think so?"

"Yes. Only my guess is that she'll try something on Sunday night. Not tonight. And not tomorrow night. I'm banking on that."

"But you're not sure?"

"No, I'm not sure. Still, this is the way I have it figured. Tonight is no good because Ken isn't here yet and nobody has taken any pictures. He'll take them tomorrow, during the day, and some more on Sunday. I've got a hunch that Ada will be wanting them all."

"But why?" Della asked. "Why this weekend, Ed?"

He smiled.

"There are a lot of reasons," he said. "I think she knows that I was the man at the window last night. Next, there—"

"How could she know?"

"I said she was smart, didn't I? Hell, you know what she did when she got back? I know. Because I sat on the porch, watching. She went over every one of those cars, putting her hand on the hoods, seeing if there was one that was warm. And she found it. Not only that, but she's been asking everybody down at the reservation if they saw me last night."

Della nodded.

"Tomorrow night she'll want to wait for more pictures on Sunday," Ed went on. "She'll want to collect as many pictures as possible for her little blackmail racket—because she may not have another chance here. With you and your husband fighting about title to the place, anything can happen."

Ed lowered his voice and spoke earnestly.

"I'mtelling you all this for just one reason. I want you to help me upset whatever her plan is, to tip it over. It's either them or me now and I want it to be me. But I need your help. Will you give it to me?"

He was a fool, she thought, a hungry, stupid fool.

"Yes," she said. "I'll help you."

"Now, I don't want to kick up any more suspicion than I have already," Ed told her. "So listen closely to what I say—"

They were interrupted by the arrival of a man and a woman,

"Hello," the man said to Ed. "Remember me?"

Ed shook his hand.

"I think you're from Red Bank."

"That's right." He nodded at the woman and winked. "My wife."

Ed smiled at the woman.

"How do you do?" he said.

The man registered, asked directions to the reservation, and the couple departed.

"He's a trap," Ed said. "He gets two or three every year."

"A trap?"

"Yes, he works on a fifty-fifty split. He picks a dame, a good sucker, and then he runs her into the camp. The one with him is pretty high in New Jersey politics. She'll pay plenty to get the negative of her picture and she won't let out a peep."

"Filthy."

Ed shrugged.

Ed went over to the window and stood there looking out.

"This is the last time," Ed told her solemnly. "There'll be no more after this. Give me tomorrow night and a month to pick up the loot and I'm out of this racket for good."

He turned around, facing her, his eyes serious.

"Know what? I'm going to buy myself a little restaurant somewhere, nothing fancy, just a little place. Then I'm going to do it over, put in some good food and live like a fellow ought to live."

"You'll never be able to wash it off," she warned him.

"Wash what off?"

"The filth."

For a moment he looked tired, older,

"You could help me, Della."

"We'll see," she said, not meaning it.

"But you'll help me?"

"I said I would."

He walked away from the window, coming over to her quickly.

"Listen to me now," he said. "You've got a watch?"

"Upstairs."

"Fine. Wear it tomorrow. Wear it all day so you don't forget it. At eight-thirty tomorrow night you come down to the reservation. Find Ken Shoals and tell him that he's got a New York call from Clifton Bradstreet. Can you remember that name?"

"I guess so."

"Well, he's one of the biggest outlets Shoals has for girlie pictures. If you remember just that, it'll be all right. But the watch is important. As soon as you have told Shoals and he has left the tent—"

"Which tent?"

"Oh. The one where we were that day." He kissed her lightly on the cheek, "I guess you'll know where that one is all right. Now, Shoals does his work behind the partition in the rear. You may have to yell for him. But he'll be there because he'll be getting his flash equipment ready to work on couples Ada will steer him to. I'll be watching for you from the other side of the field. After Shoals leaves the tent to answer the phone you walk straight across the clearing. The reason for this is that I may not be able to recognize him at that distance but I'll be able to spot your blonde hair. As soon as you do this, I'll go over to the tent Shoals just left."

Another man and woman came in, registered and left.

"By this time it will be getting close to dusk," Ed went on. "Wait until Shoals has started for the house, then get your clothes from the women's tent. Carry them with you and go back to the tent Shoals was working in. Go inside and put on your clothes. Hide behind some of the boxes if you want to. But keep your eye on your watch. At a quarter of nine you will hear someone yell 'Fire.' When you hear that go to the back of the tent and pick up the green hatbox sitting on the ground right in the middle of his equipment. Go out the back way, into the woods, and keep going. Circle the field and come back to the house. Hide the box where it can't be found. And wait for me. I'll join you as soon as I can."

It sounded easy, Della thought. Nothing to it.

"And the fire?" she inquired.

"Aw, hell, it'll be just a little blaze that I'll start. I'll burn a handful of film and after it's over nobody'll be hurt and nobody'll know what caused it."

"It sounds all right," she said.

"Solid."

"Only one weak point, Ed."

"Yeah?"

"Me." She smiled at him. "I'll have the box. How do you know you can trust me?"

He lowered his head and brushed his lips across her mouth.

"I think I can. I have to trust somebody."

"But you're not sure."

"No," he admitted. "I'm not sure." He reached into a pocket and brought out an envelope. "I forgot to add something, Della. No matter what happens afterward between you and me—even if I don't ever see you again—when I get the box we make an exchange. You get the negative of your picture."

"Thank you," she said as a car drove up. "Now I know the deal."

"We both know."

Another car rumbled up the driveway.

"Until tomorrow night," Ed said.

She walked to the door.

"Until tomorrow night," she said.

At six, Della and Jennie had supper in the kitchen.

"Fish," Della said. "Cod. I used to help dry this stuff back in Iceland."

"It's good," Jennie said.

You wouldn't think so, Della decided, not if you lived near the fields where they hung it out like tobacco in the sun. Sometimes at night the wind would shift and you'd have to put your window down or you'd get so sick you wouldn't be able to eat for a week.

"You can have tomorrow night off," Della told the girl. "Say, from about seven on."

"Thanks, Mrs. Farland."

"But I want the car left here."

The smile disappeared from Jennie's face.

"Gee, Mrs. Farland, I don't know. Sammy works until—"

"I'll pay your cab fare. Don't worry about that."

Jennie piled the dishes near the sink, got the Rinso out and started the water.

"You've sure changed since Mr. Farland hasn't been around," Jennie observed.

Della hesitated in the doorway, considering the statement.

"I believe I have," she admitted.

The last car arrived about nine but she waited an other half hour before leaving the porch and going in side. The sounds of music and laughter drifted up from the reservation, filling the night. In a few days, a few hours perhaps, tears of desperation would replace the laughter of some of these people. It was a bitter, hard world.

She had just turned on the cellar light when someone knocked on the kitchen door. It was Ken Shoals.

"Only giving you the word," he said. "I'm staying down below. I got a feeling my equipment will be safer down there."

She nodded and watched his back disappear into the darkness. She wondered, without caring, if he enjoyed his work.

The cellar was as modern as the rest of the house, though she hadn't used it very much. Ricky had explained once, laughingly, that the cellar belonged to him and she could have the balance of the place. She had supposed, at the time, that it was because he'd kept his liquor down there.

The walls were finished off in knotty pine and at the far end, in one corner, was a serving bar. Behind this stood a huge three-cornered cabinet where Ricky had kept his golf clubs, fishing equipment and guns. She hoped that he hadn't cleaned everything out.

The fishing equipment, she soon discovered, was gone. So were the golf clubs and the hunting bow with the sixtypound pull, And the rifles and the shotguns, these had been taken away, too.

Della swore and jerked the drawers open, one after the other. Nothing. She swore again. Then, in a shallow walnut case, she found what she wanted. The gun.

So he had not bothered to take it. Good. She lifted it out of the case, A thirty-two Smith and Wesson.

Deadly, Ricky had once explained to her. Small and deadly. Her hand broke the gun open and she spun the cylinder. Loaded. Six bullets.

When she got back to the bedroom she tried the gun on for size. It wouldn't work with the white halter but if she wore the red one, the one with the wire and fringes at the top; she could carry the gun in that, between her breasts. She stood before the mirror, turning slowly. The bulge was noticeable but in the late hours of evening no one would see it. No one would see it unless she took it out and pointed it at them.

She hid the gun in one of the bureau drawers and undressed for bed. As she crossed the room to open the window she passed in front of the mirror. She glanced at herself. Beautiful, she thought, a truly beautiful body. The naked body of a woman. "No artist could capture it," Ricky had told her once, long ago. "They could put it on canvas but they couldn't make it live, make it glow—not the way you glow."

A sob came into her throat as she stood remembering.

"The easiest," Ed Loring had told her. "The easiest I ever had."

She wanted to be sick. She wanted to throw something at the mirror and smash it.

In bed, with the lights out, she cried. She was being weak when she should be strong, displaying fear when she should be courageous.

She rolled over, closing her eyes. It was a good thing that she'd found the gun. She'd have gotten drunk or gone out of her mind or done something terrible if she hadn't. She hadn't been thinking of it, not actually, but the night before was still with her, those moments in Ricky's motel room still haunting her. There was nothing for them now, never again, not for her and Ricky. And Ed. Ed was worse. Ed wasn't fighting for anything that belonged to him; he was just fighting for money to steal.

Sounds of the music floated up from the lake. It was an old song, *I'm in the Mood for Love*. Della turned over again, twisting the sheet around her and pulling the pillow over her head.

13

EIGHT TWENTY-FIVE. Eight twenty-five, Della thought, on Saturday this side of hell.

She walked across the field through the gathering dusk, her body naked except for the shoes and the cap.

The shoes were comfortable but the cap hurt. Underneath the cap was the gun.

Nakedness was everywhere. Men and women, talking, laughing, joking. A radio blared, giving the lineup of the Dodgers for the night game. Then the radio faded and a battery of violins took up a Viennese waltz.

"Wonderful place," a fat man said.

It stinks, Della thought.

"A paradise," another man said. "Real outdoors."

Della reached the tent and stopped.

"Mr. Shoals." She pulled the flap aside. "Mr Shoals!"

"Yeah?"

The tent was lighted with a small yellow bulb. The voice came from beyond the canvas partition.

"There's a phone call for you. Long distance. Some man by the name of Bradstreet wants to talk to you."

The partition parted and Ken Shoals stepped out. He too was naked and he looked a lot worse with his clothes off than he did with them on.

"Aw, for gosh sakes," he complained. "I wonder what he wants."

Della managed a smile.

"He said he wanted you."

Ken Shoals turned away.

"Tell him I'll call him back."

She waited a second and then gave him the hook.

"He's hanging on," Della said. "I'm sure it's important."

The photographer hesitated a moment, then made his way toward her,

"Hell," he said. "Most likely a lot of bother over nothing."

He came out of the tent and stood looking at her.

"You've got some shape," he told her. "Nice." He laughed, walking away.

She followed him across the clearing and hurried into the women's tent. She was grateful for the fact that no one else was in there. Quickly she pulled on her shorts, tied the halter in place and pushed the gun down in the front. Then she went outside and waited, the metal of the gun digging into her breasts. It was so dark now no one could tell whether she was dressed or not.

Ken Shoals appeared in a few moments and walked to the trees, disappearing into the darkness.

Deliberately she turned and walked across the field again. There was a dull roar in her head and her mouth was parched and dry. She glanced at the watch as she reached the tent. It was twenty minutes before nine.

Inside, she tied the straps on the flaps securely before going on through past the partition. Another yellow light burned in there.

The green box was not in the middle of the floor.

She moved around the tiny space, hunting. There were photos and film all over. She found a box and started to gather them up. Almost instantly, she stopped and threw the box down. This was no mistake. This was deliberate. Ed had gotten the pictures he wanted, and he was gone. Ed had used her for a decoy to get Ken Shoals away from the tent.

Somehow, she was not surprised, nor was she angry. It was part of the fast and deadly game they were playing.

She found a piece of newspaper and rumpled it, laying it close to a pile of the film. Then she took a book of matches from her pocket, struck one and held it. Maybe she wouldn't be able to burn them all, as she had intended doing, but she would get some of them. There were a lot of faces in those pictures, a lot of faces of people who wouldn't have to pay. She touched the match to the paper.

Moving quickly, she slipped through the opening at the rear of the tent, stumbled once over a stake, recovered and started running toward the woods. Once in the woods she stopped and looked back.

"Fire!" somebody was shouting. "Fire! Fire!"

She looked at the tent. An orange glow had appeared inside, wavering, but as yet it was the only visible sign of fire. Glancing to the right she saw the red blaze of flames leaping skyward and the naked figures moving around it.

"Damn!"

She swung further away from the clearing, deeper into the woods. Something had gone wrong. Maybe Ed hadn't gotten to the tent. Maybe there weren't any other pictures. She hoped there weren't. But there was at least one more. The one Ed had, the photo of herself. She had to find Ed.

The gun was in her hand, small and deadly. She began running again. The scrub oaks dug into her legs and small stinging branches whipped her across the face. Once she struck a tree and fell down. She got up, gasping for breath. She didn't care. Nothing mattered except one thing. She had to find Ed.

Wild shouts went up from the clearing. She glanced back. Red flames were' shooting into the sky. She laughed and kept on running.

Minutes later she came out of the woods. Her breasts ached and she was so exhausted that she wanted to lie down. But she couldn't. She had to go on. She had to get to the house. Had to be there when Ed arrived. If he would arrive.

She reached the house but she didn't go inside. She clung to the railing on the back steps, fighting for breath, conscious now of the pain in her legs, the awful, hollow ache in her chest. Every breath was an effort preceded by a thought. She remembered something that Ricky had told her one time when they'd been swimming. Don't think about it, he'd said; don't think about breathing and you can stay underwater twice as long. Think about something else, he'd said. Yes, think about Ed and the pictures and what was happening down there.

She sat down on the steps, waiting, the gun in her hand. The shouts were still coming up from the reservation but had subsided somewhat. The fire no longer lit the sky. She continued to wait, breathing steadily now, feeling sore all over.

A figure moved up the road, coming fast. The white shirt appeared as though it were a ghost walking on top of nothing.

She waited until he was close to the porch.

"Ed?"

"Della! Christ, what happened?"

She stood up, the gun leveled at his shirt.

"I burned your pretty pictures," she told him. "Aren't I awful?"

The shirt stood still briefly, then moved toward her.

"You lousy bitch!"

"I have a gun here," Della said. She was surprised that her voice was so calm. "If you come one step closer I'll kill you, Ed."

"You must be crazy," he said. But he remained motionless.

"Crazy enough to kill you, yes."

"Bitch," he said. "I should have known better."

She laughed at him.

"You have my picture and I have the gun. I'll make a trade with you, Ed. I'll save one of my bullets if you give me the picture."

"And if I don't."

She laughed at him again.

"I'll just need one shot."

The shirt moved as he shifted his weight from one foot to the other. She could barely see the outline of his face.

"You could have brought the box," he said in disgust. "That was the deal."

"It wasn't there."

"Like hell it wasn't!"

"But I'm telling you it wasn't!"

The night came in around them, bringing them very close for a hushed instant.

"It must have been Ada," he whispered in disbelief. "She guessed what we were up to. Damn her."

"Shut up, Ed, and give me the picture."

"But it was Ada!"

"I don't care who it was. Give me the picture."

He came slowly toward her and stopped.

"Here it is," Ed said. "It's yours. Nothing went right but I'll admit you earned it."

She reached for the white envelope in his hand.

"Thanks, Ed."

He moved fast, cursing savagely, and she had no time to shoot. He twisted her arm up high and to the rear, toppling her to the steps.

Then he was on top of her, his knee punching her in the stomach, the pain going all the way to her back.

"You've got the picture," he yelled at her. "Gimme the gun! All I want is the gun!"

"No!"

He twisted her arm again, down along her side. She tried to lift her leg to kick him but she couldn't. Her free hand went to his face, digging the nails into his skin, cutting him. The gun kept going down and down.

She screamed once as he turned and bit her on the hand and the gun went off.

"Christ," he said.

He got up. The gun rattled down the steps and he grabbed it.

"The bitch," he said. "I'll kill her!"

"Ed!"

"I'll kill her!"

She sat up. A sharp pain shot through her right leg.

"No, Ed!"

But he was already gone, running down the road, cursing violently.

The envelope was there on the bottom step. She picked it up and tore it into tiny pieces. When she looked at her hands she saw that they were covered with blood.

She stood up, trembling. She felt of her right leg, moving down from the top, and when she reached the calf there was the blood and there was the hole. She limped slowly toward the car.

If she could get it started, she thought, climbing in. How did you get one of these things going? She closed her eyes, remembering how Jennie did it. Her hand found the key and she turned it. The other hand found the starter button, pressed hard. The engine roared and she took a deep breath. The lights. Where the hell were the lights? She pulled on one knob and the car almost stalled. She pulled another and the lights came on. The gears ground and the car began to move forward.

She tried to think. There were a lot of things that she had to do. The police, she had to get them. She should have called the police from the house. But she hadn't. She supposed it didn't make much difference. Ed would do what he had set out to do. It was too late to stop him.

She came to a turn in the road and almost lost control of the car before she found the brake. The tires squealed and the wooden body creaked.

When she reached the highway she turned right, toward the Landing, driving as fast as she dared. Hell, she thought, there's nothing to handling a car in the States. She should have been doing it a long time ago.

She came to a bridge, crossed it and started up a short, steep hill. The headlights of an approaching car probed the night. Part way up the hill the car broke into view, moving fast. For a moment the lights blinded her and her left foot sought the dimmer switch. And it was then that she knew, knew with terrifying certainty, that there would be an accident, that she was driving the Ford on the wrong side of the road.

The onrushing car lurched, its tires screaming on the macadam. She felt the Ford sway drunkenly as she spun the wheel, heard the scrape of metal on stone as the car plowed into the bank. Her foot slammed down hard on the brake, slipped off and slammed down again. She was thrown forward against the steering wheel, then back against the seat as the station wagon jolted to a halt.

"God," she whispered.

She looked out and down. The road seemed far below.

The other car was down there, far over on the shoulder of the highway, its motor running. In the distance a siren wailed.

"Hey, up there! You okay?"

It was Ricky.

"I'm all right," she said.

He got out of the car, stood there in the road, laughing at her.

"I should have known it," he said. "Only a dumb mojack would be driving on the wrong side of the road. This is the States, baby. You drive on the right-hand side down here."

She was furious with him.

"Never mind," she told him as he started up the bank. She pushed the door open and got out of the car. "I can manage by myself."

Her leg pained when she put her weight on it and there was so much drying blood in her sandal that it felt as though she were standing in wet sand.

"Just a minute," Ricky told her.

A police car came into view, siren screaming. It slowed, coming down the hill, and stopped near Ricky. The police and Ricky talked for a moment and then the police car moved, on, gathering speed.

"I said to wait, didn't I?" Ricky demanded. "I never saw anybody so stubborn as an Icelander."

She was by the side of the road now, barely able to stand, her leg throbbing.

"Cripes!" Ricky exclaimed, coming closer. "Look at your leg, baby!"

She tried to smile.

"You look at it," she said weakly. "I'm sick of it already."

He picked her up, lifting her in his strong arms, and it seemed so good not to have to stand anymore.

"What happened, baby?"

"I had a gun and it went off."

He carried her over to the Caddy.

"Accidentally?"

"I was fighting with Ed Loring."

He opened the door with one hand and placed her gently on the seat.

"And what happened to him?"

"He took the gun away from me." She felt so tired and she wanted to forget about all of it. "I think he was going to kill Ada Holden."

Ricky closed the door, crossed in front of the headlights, and got in behind the wheel.

"I wish him good hunting," Ricky said.

The engine of the Caddy roared and he swung the car around quickly, heading back toward the Landing.

"He kills her and he'll burn," Ricky assured her. "The cops will have him before he can get to the main road. They'll both get what they ought to get."

She held her leg out straight, half sitting on the seat. There was less discomfort that way.

"The police," Della said. "I don't understand about them."

They came to a sharp curve but Ricky never slowed the big car.

"I went and got them."

"You?"

"Yes." He glanced at her, smiling a little. "After Thursday night—say, was that Ed Loring at the window?"

She nodded.

"Well, I didn't know, but I guessed as much. Anyway, after Thursday night, after you'd gone, I had quite a talk with Ada. She was—upset. I got the idea that it wasn't so much that they wanted to stay out at the

Nest forever as it was to have something so conclusive on the owner that the owner would never talk about their blackmail racket."

"Ricky—"

"Let me finish, will you? I'm only trying to say that after you left I sort of gave her the idea that I'd get the property away from you anyhow. You see, when I first met her, down in the hotel bar, that was the thing she wanted to talk to me about, whether you owned the Nest or I owned it. At first, I thought it was pretty silly—what difference did it make, they were there, weren't they? But later, the other night, she told me that she wanted to cut out this Ed Loring. She wanted a permanent location; she was tired of jumping around all over. When I couldn't convince her that I'd get it away from you and she got the idea I might go to the police, she showed me a little picture."

Della shut her eyes.

"Of—me?"

"No. Ricky Farland. Me. Me and her. She must have had it taken the first night she was out to the motel, but—"

"I'm sorry, Ricky. It's been an awful mess."

He lit two cigarettes and handed one to her. "Ada made a mistake when she came up with that picture of me. Oh, I got that one from her all right—I just took it—but, of course, there was the negative. The next day I went to the police. They did some checking and found out that this crew is vicious. When Ada told me that you were going to hang onto the property, she said she had a film that would make you change your mind. The cops told me to let her use it, to use you as bait, but when Ed got there, before they did, and took the film—well, that ruined things. I told them I'd keep on things and let them know when to hit the camp."

The lights of the Landing shown in the distance.

Ricky grinned and puffed on a cigarette.

"Now I'll tell you something else. I was there," he said. "I was smelling around. And I confiscated a green box."

In a way, she wasn't surprised.

"I followed you," he explained. "I followed you when you left the house. When you went in that tent to take off your clothes I took mine off in the woods. When you walked over to tell that fellow about the phone call I kept about twenty-five feet in back of you. After you had both gone I went into that tent, not to look for anything exactly but to have some place to hide and study out the situation. I saw a green box in plain sight, a box filled with pictures, and I decided then that something was up. So I dumped out the box, looking for the negative of my own picture, but I didn't find it. When I heard someone coming I shoved most of the photos back into the box and went out the back. A couple of minutes later somebody yelled 'Fire!' and I decided it was time to move. I got over to my clothes, put them on and ran up to the house. The police were waiting along the road, back there a ways, and I came down for them."

Ricky, she thought, you foolhardy idiot, you could have been killed.

"What happened to the pictures?"

"I gave them to the police. They'll be used as evidence but none of them will be made public. The people who were guests will not be injured in any way and their names will not be used. From now on they may have sense enough to go to only those nudist camps that are approved."

She told him then about Ed Loring's plans, what she had done and what had happened.

"Never mind. We've got to get you to a doctor," Ricky said.

The lights of the town moved closer and up ahead a red light blinker poked its finger into the night.

"We got off on the wrong foot, baby," Ricky said. "Too much of nothing and not enough of the things that counted. Too much booze at the start because I was scared of losing you, too much of it later on because I thought I had."

Della closed her eyes.

"Let's not fight," she whispered.

She felt the car slow, his arm go around her shoulder.

"I'm not fighting. I'm talking. I'm trying to say that we've both been wrong, that we've both made mistakes. I'm trying to say that I thought I hated you but I don't any more. I don't know if I love you or if I don't. But I do know some other things. I know that I haven't got a dime. I know that we've both done a lot of harm to ourselves and that we've lost a lot of friends."

She opened her eyes, watching him.

"Yes, Ricky."

His hand tightened on her shoulder.

"What I'm trying to say is this—I've got nobody and you've got nobody. We were happy once. Why don't we try to be that way again?"

Ricky, she thought, Ricky, you're trying to start it all over again.

"There's Jennie," she reminded him, "We have to think of her."

"All right. We'll think about her."

"At least, the baby."

"Yes."

"We could help her. And—well, if it's too much for her later on, if she feels—"

"We could adopt it," Ricky suggested.

Della closed her eyes again, closed them against the tears.

"Yes," she said. "We could adopt it."

They stopped at a traffic light and the motor idled smoothly.

"You won't hold it against me, baby?"

"No." She couldn't be sure.

He leaned over and kissed her on the mouth as the light changed.

"I think I love you, Della," he said. "But ease your mind. That baby isn't mine. Probably it belongs to that Sammy of hers."

"Jennie lied?" she gasped. "Is that what you're telling me?"

"I don't blame her," he said. "Possibly you made the opening. You were only too ready to believe the worst about me, so she went along with the gag—out of some vague notion of pleasing you, or improving the lot of her child, safeguarding its future—"

The car stopped and she went into his arms, her leg paining fiercely,

"Ricky. Oh, Ricky, forgive me!"

He kissed her.

"We haven't got a dime," he said. "Not a dime."

"Don't worry about it. Ricky, we'll get by."

He stroked her hair and looked down into her eyes.

"I thought of something real crazy," he said. "We've got the tents up there and we've done a good turn for the nudists by getting rid of those crumbs. The nudists will respect us after this. Why don't we run a real camp for them? An honest one."

She kissed him on the lips.

"I'd like it fine," she said.

"They'll gossip about us, anyway."

"I know."

"But what do we care?"

Her arms went around him and she told him it didn't matter, didn't matter at all.

"Where are we?" she wanted to know.

"At Doc Anderson's," he said. He got out and walked around the car. "It's about the only place we can charge a medical bill at this time of the night."

He picked her up and carried her toward the house. When he reached the door he hesitated, grinned, and then kissed her good and hard.

"We'll get over it," he promised her.

Della Farland nodded and clung to her husband.

It was a chance they had to take.

WOLFBAIT
UNDER THE COUNTER CULTURE

ALSO AVAILABLE BY ORRIE HITT

The Naked Flesh
A novel of sun-soaked sin and small-town secrets!

THE STEPHEN GLASS COLLECTION

Amazons of Yesteryear
A rare, action-packed collection of images of
wrestling women of the 1940s and 1950s.

Beauty Off-Duty
Relaxed, everyday moments caught on camera.

Naked in the Menagerie
A playful look at Eve accompanied by her animal friends.

Nudist Camp Follies – volumes 1 and 2
An intimate look at the natural and free atmosphere in Sun Clubs.

Nymphs and Naiads
Beauty unadorned and outdoors.

Poise and Pose
A magnificent series of photographs
of female beauty taken in the studio.

THE EVA GRANT COLLECTION

The Glamour Camera of Eva Grant

A short biography of Eva Grant, one of the world's foremost female
figure photographers of the 1950s and 1960s, accompanied by a
selection of some of her most enticing work.

Line and Form

A nostalgic review of Eva Grant's glamour magazine of the 1950s.

Glamour Model Revue

Featuring June Palmer, Paula Page and Tina Madison.

THE WILLIAM WELBY COLLECTION

Naked and Unashamed:

Nudism from Six Points of View.
William Welby's initial impressions of nudism.

The Naked Truth about Nudism

William Welby gets to bare all in this
first hand exploration of British Naturism.

It's Only Natural: The Philosophy of Nudism

William Welby's musings on getting back to nature
and the tyranny of fashion.

OTHER TITLES

Naked as Nature Intended
The epic tale of a nudist picture by Pamela Green,
with photographs by Douglas "Dambuster" Webb, DFM.

The Naked Truth About Harrison Marks
The notorious biography by Franklyn Wood.

Slide Show
A luscious look at the photographic
slides of Harrison Marks.

Past Masters of the Nude
An illustrated bibliography of nude photography books
published in England from 1896 to 1960.

Doing Rude Things
The history of the British sex film.

Cinema au Naturel
A history of nudist film.

Sauna for Beginners
A Pocket Guide.

Miniten: Rules of the Game
Invented in the 1930s, Miniten is a
tennis-like game played by naturists.

X-ray Specs and Other Vintage Ads
A unique treasure chest of vintage advertising,
full of tease and prurient silliness.

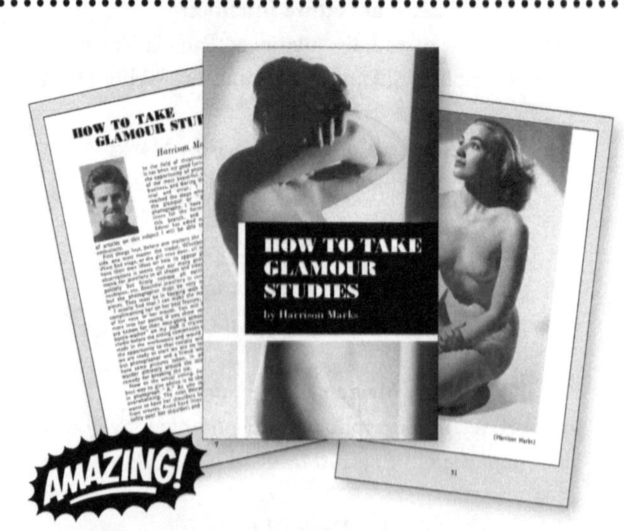

9 781917 298070